AVENGING ANGEL

He jumped down to the ground, and was rounding the wagon when he heard what sounded like a struggle, followed by the wounded Mexican's sharp, strangled cry. Longarm turned around and clambered swiftly back up into the wagon. Consuela, Longarm's bloody pocket knife in her hand, was standing over the young Mexican. He was flat on his back now, a bloody ribbon under his chin where Consuela had slit his throat. From the slit, his dark blood had poured out onto the bed of the wagon. There was no doubt about it. He was dead . . .

Also in the LONGARM series from Jove

- LONGARM
- LONGARM AND THE LONE STAR LEGEND
- LONGARM AND THE LONE STAR BOUNTY
- LONGARM AND THE LONE STAR RUSTLERS
- LONGARM AND THE LONE STAR DELIVERANCE
- LONGARM IN THE TEXAS PANHANDLE
- LONGARM AND THE RANCHER'S SHOWDOWN
- LONGARM ON THE INLAND PASSAGE
- LONGARM IN THE RUBY RANGE COUNTRY
- LONGARM AND THE GREAT CATTLE KILL
- LONGARM AND THE CROOKED RAILMAN
- LONGARM ON THE SIWASH TRAIL
- LONGARM AND THE RUNAWAY THIEVES
- LONGARM AND THE ESCAPE ARTIST
- LONGARM IN THE BIG BURNOUT
- LONGARM AND THE TREACHEROUS TRIAL
- LONGARM AND THE NEW MEXICO SHOOT-OUT
- LONGARM AND THE LONE STAR FRAME
- LONGARM AND THE RENEGADE SERGEANT
- LONGARM IN THE SIERRA MADRES
- LONGARM AND THE MEDICINE WOLF
- LONGARM AND THE INDIAN RAIDERS
- LONGARM IN A DESERT SHOWDOWN
- LONGARM AND THE MAD DOG KILLER
- LONGARM AND THE HANGMAN'S NOOSE
- LONGARM AND THE REBEL KILLERS
- LONGARM AND THE HANGMAN'S LIST
- LONGARM IN THE CLEARWATERS
- LONGARM AND THE REDWOOD RAIDERS
- LONGARM AND THE DEADLY JAILBREAK
- LONGARM AND THE PAWNEE KID
- LONGARM AND THE DEVIL'S STAGECOACH
- LONGARM AND THE WYOMING BLOODBATH
- LONGARM IN THE RED DESERT
- LONGARM AND THE CROOKED MARSHAL
- LONGARM AND THE TEXAS RANGERS
- LONGARM AND THE VIGILANTES
- LONGARM IN THE OSAGE STRIP
- LONGARM AND THE LOST MINE
- LONGARM AND THE LONGLEY LEGEND
- LONGARM AND THE DEAD MAN'S BADGE
- LONGARM AND THE KILLER'S SHADOW
- LONGARM AND THE MONTANA MASSACRE
- LONGARM IN THE MEXICAN BADLANDS
- LONGARM AND THE BOUNTY HUNTRESS
- LONGARM AND THE DENVER BUSTOUT
- LONGARM AND THE SKULL CANYON GANG
- LONGARM AND THE RAILROAD TO HELL
- LONGARM AND THE LONE STAR CAPTIVE
- LONGARM AND THE RIVER OF DEATH

TABOR EVANS

LONGARM
AND THE GOLD HUNTERS

JOVE BOOKS, NEW YORK

LONGARM AND THE GOLD HUNTERS

A Jove Book / published by arrangement with
the author

PRINTING HISTORY
Jove edition / September 1991

All rights reserved.
Copyright © 1991 by Jove Publications, Inc.
This book may be not be reproduced in whole
or in part, by mimeograph or any other means,
without permission. For information address:
The Berkley Publishing Group, 200 Madison Avenue,
New York, New York 10016.

ISBN: 0-515-10669-0

Jove Books are published by The Berkley Publishing Group,
200 Madison Avenue, New York, New York 10016.
The name "JOVE" and the "J" logo
are trademarks belonging to Jove Publications, Inc.

PRINTED IN THE UNITED STATES OF AMERICA

10 9 8 7 6 5 4 3 2 1

LONGARM
AND THE GOLD HUNTERS

Chapter 1

It was as black as a whore's heart when Longarm left the Windsor Hotel. The night was threatening rain, but that threat had been an empty one for some time now. For two days the clouds had been piling in from the west with the sultry heat building under them. The Mile High City's inhabitants were trapped in a huge Turkish bath with the Devil himself piling on the coal. The gaslit street lamps floated in a glowing bubble of humidity, emitting a light so feeble that sidewalks, buildings, even the lampposts themselves, lacked any real solidity—while the few men and women still abroad took on the aspect of troubled spirits trapped in a grim netherworld.

Tugging his hat down more firmly, Longarm flung away his cheroot and stepped carefully off the sidewalk onto the street's manure-slicked cobblestones. He was halfway across it when a ghostly hack bore down on him out of the shrouded night, only to veer away at the last moment, the hackie's disembodied curse floating eerily back to him as he continued on across the street.

A moment later, as he strode down a narrow sidestreet, a shortcut he usually took on his way back to his Cherry Street rooming house, he found himself mulling over the poker game he had just left. He had cashed in after pocketing more than thirty dollars, and the look on the faces of his three poker partners had reflected more than dismay at his abrupt decision to pack it in for the night. Their discomfiture did not bother him in the least. The three men had no manners. They talked too loudly, spat carelessly in the direction of the cuspidors, and cried out gleefully and slapped each other on the back whenever one of them managed a winning hand. All in all, they resembled three baying hounds who had somehow managed the astounding trick of sitting upright on chairs so they could play poker.

Shaking his head at the thought, he moved on down the narrow, fog-shrouded street with a ground-devouring, catlike stride. The few men he encountered ducked hastily aside as he loomed toward them out of the steaming gloom. A huge Belgian workhorse standing in the traces of a beer wagon materialized at the curb beside him. Longarm increased his pace just in time as the horse sent a thick, steaming gout of urine pounding onto the fresh manure between its feet.

A second later, above the gush of the urine's hard splatter, he thought he heard a cry from behind him.

He chuckled. Some poor fool must've gotten caught.

He glanced back. Two shadowy figures jumped away from the horse and into a doorway. Without pause, Longarm turned back around and continued on. The night was not dark enough to keep him from recognizing the men. They were two of his three poker partners.

He increased his pace, determined to pick his own time and place for what was afoot. He crossed the Colfax Avenue bridge, and was crunching along the damp cinder path on the other side when he glanced back and saw that the two were following him more boldly now, making no effort to hide their intentions from him. The taller of the two called himself Lars Peterson; the other one was Hake Haskins, a heavier, more truculent sort. The third one, a smaller gent they called Amos, was nowhere it sight. He was nearby, though; Longarm had no doubt of that.

He waved to them. They did not wave back, just kept on, the two of them glowering at him.

Sore losers.

A block from his rooming house, Longarm ducked into a familiar alley and loped around the building, coming out on the sidewalk behind the two men. They were in front of him now, peering cautiously into the mouth of the alley. Longarm ran silently toward them. Only at the last moment did the two hear him and spin around to face him. But Longarm was already between them. He planted a solid punch on Peterson's chops and the man went down like a sack of potatoes.

Haskins backed away, crouching, a sap in his right hand, its leather cover gleaming. Lunging suddenly forward, Haskins swung out at Longarm, the sap slicing the air inches from his chin. Ducking low, Longarm stepped inside Haskins's guard, grabbed his wrist with both hands, and twisted. Crying out, Haskins dropped the sap. Longarm flung the man back, then swept up the sap and went after Haskins. Backing up, Haskins was reaching inside his coat for a weapon when Longarm swung the sap and caught him with cruel precision, the ball bearings inside the sap smashing Haskins flush on the side of his face. The cheekbone shattered under the blow and Haskins spun off the sidewalk and collapsed facedown in the gutter, his nose plowing up fresh horse manure.

Longarm stepped back and looked around. Where was Amos, the third one?

He heard pounding feet behind him, whirled, and saw the little fat man running off down the street. In a moment, his pudgy form had vanished into the gloom. Longarm stepped over the barely conscious Peterson and continued on to his rooming house. The tension built up by this encounter with his two ex-poker partners was still with him when he pushed open the door and entered his room. He walked over to his dresser, lit the lamp on it, then turned to his bed—and found himself staring into the bore of a huge Remington revolver. Behind this cannon was a dark-eyed Mexican woman with near-ebony hair, olive complexion, and a cleft deep enough to bivouac an army. Her red blouse was cut low; her green, red-trimmed skirt reached only to her ankles, revealing her high-topped patent-leather shoes.

"You are the Longarm?" she asked.

"Yes. I am the Longarm."

Slowly she lowered the revolver.

He reached out and gently removed it from her grasp. "That's one hell of a way to greet a man."

"I did not know if it was you."

"It's me, all right. Custis Long is my legal name. And who might you be?"

"I am Consuela."

"What's all this about, Consuela?"

"I need your help."

"What kind?"

"My man, he is dead. Now three men—they come after me."

"Why?"

"I have the map."

"Map? What map?"

"The one to show where the gold is hid."

Longarm held up his hand. "Look, why don't we just turn around and start all over." As he spoke, he dropped her revolver into his top bureau drawer. "I don't know what the hell you're talking about."

"First you must swear to protect me."

"From who?"

"From the three men who want the gold."

Longarm sighed. "What gold, Consuela?"

Her dark, luminous eyes lit up then and the tip of her tongue peeked out from her bold lips. "The gold my man steal."

"Your man?"

"Ortega Gasset," she said proudly, her eyes glowing.

Longarm recalled the man instantly. A few months before, he had delivered Gasset to the Yuma prison.

"You say Ortega's hid some gold away?"

"Yes!"

"And you have the map to show where it is?"

She nodded.

"Can I see it?"

"Do you swear on the grave of your mother to protect me from those three who pursue me?"

"You have my word."

"You swear too easy, I think."

"So far, Consuela, all you've done is talk. If you've got a map that shows where this gold is stashed, show it to me."

"All right," she said. "I think maybe I will trust you."

She stepped back, lifted her blouse over her head, and flung it aside. Then she stepped out of her skirt. As he had surmised, there had been no slips or pantaloons under it. He was astonished. Her hour-glass figure needed no corset to hold in her waist or lift her magnificent breasts. Between her ample thighs, her gleaming pubic hair was thick, luxuriant, its dark strands coiling clear up to her navel.

Abruptly she turned around and bent forward over the bed, presenting her ample cheeks to him.

Longarm was puzzled. "You want me to kick you," he said. "That it?"

"No, you gringo fool! Can't you see?"

"Consuela, straighten up and turn back around. I know I sound like a crank, but that's not the way I prefer it."

Cursing in lovely accented Spanish, she flung herself forward onto the bed, then turned her head to regard him, her dark eyes blazing.

"On my *cheeks*," she hissed. "Look for yourself."

With a frown he approached the bed and leaned over to gaze at her dusky half-moons—and saw at once what she meant. A map had been tattooed on the lower flanks of each cheek. Placing his big hands on her silken skin, he pressed the cheeks together. The map joined and became an eloquent testimonial to the talent of whoever had wielded the tattoo needle. Towns, rivers, even the location of peaks stood out clearly—including the canyon where the gold was supposedly hidden, apparently some distance from the town of Needle Gap.

"Now," she said, turning on her side, "do you understan'?"

He sat down on the edge of the bed beside her, finding it increasingly difficult to concentrate on the business at hand. "I understand, all right. But how the hell did that map get there?"

"I was very drunk. Ortega, he tell me he want to tattoo his name on my pretty ass. He do this, he say, so if he go to prison no one will dare sleep with me."

"I didn't see his name there."

"I know that now. I not know it then."

"What do you mean?"

"How could I see it? Do you know what is written on *your* ass? I still cannot see it myself—until I hold mirror between my legs, and still I cannot read what it say."

"So when did you find out what was there?"

"When the three men who escape from Yuma with him come to my place and tell me Ortega is dead. The guards shoot him and he die, but they escape and come to find me. Then they take me. After they do this, they turn me over to copy the map. They leave with only the little short man to watch me. I hit him with rifle barrel, then I throw the map they make in the fire. Then I come here to you."

"Why me?"

"Ortega, he tell me about you."

Longarm nodded. In a way, he had been sorry to hear the outlaw was dead. It had taken a while for Longarm to track Ortega, and while he was bringing him in, he'd gotten a chance to know the outlaw and had come to hold a grudging respect for him. The two men had swapped stories of their escapades, and Longarm had been sorry when he heard the length of the sentence the judge had given him. Well, it looked like the poor son of a bitch was out of it now.

"I remember Ortega," Longarm said to Consuela, his hand resting on her dusky thigh. It was almost searing to the touch. "I'm sorry to hear he is dead."

She rested her hand on his. "He tell me you are one fair lawman. He also tell me you are the best man he ever know with gun. So I come to you. I do not want them three cockroaches to get the gold."

"Consuela, how much gold are we talking about, and where did it come from?"

"I do not know that," she said. "Besides, it does not matter. There is much gold, I promise you. Now, will you help me?"

He gazed at her speculatively, wondering just how much to believe. "There's something you should know," he told her.

"What ees that?"

"I think I met your three buddies on the way here."

Her eyes narrowed. "You met them?"

"It was more of a collision. What I want to know is how they knew enough to come after me."

"I was fool. When they rape me, I scream at them. I tell them I am your friend and that you will avenge me. They know of you. Ortega, he tell them in Yuma prison what a man you are. So now maybe they try to keep you from helping me, I think."

"Mentioning me was a fool thing to do."

"Next time, you tell me how to think clear while I am raped," she snapped, her eyes flashing angrily.

"Sorry."

"I forgive you." She smiled suddenly, brilliantly. "Is it deal?"

"It's a deal."

"You go with me to get the gold?"

"I already told you I would."

"And then we will be very rich!"

"If the gold's there."

"It is there. Trust me. So now, get undressed."

He did so, and quickly. She opened her arms to him and spread her thighs eagerly. He plunged deep and felt her shuddering sigh. Her long legs swung up to scissor his waist, and in a moment he was plunging headlong into her sweet oblivion.

Vail cocked an eyebrow at Longarm.

"What's this? You want a week off?"

"Maybe two."

Vail was mopping his brow. "Out with it. What's up?"

"You remember Ortega Gasset?"

"Yeah, I remember." Vail reached for a jug of water on his desk and filled his glass. "You should too. You brought him in."

"He's dead. Died escaping from Yuma. I met his woman late last night. She's the one told me."

"Ortega's woman?"

"You heard me."

"And she spent the night with you?"

"It was a dark, miserable night—and she had nowhere else to go."

"You devil."

"Anyway, as I understand it, we hauled Ortega in for a stagecoach robbery. Right?"

"So?"

"He insisted he had not robbed it."

"That's what the poor son of a bitch said, all right."

"Well, he pretty near convinced me."

Vail shrugged. "What difference does it make if he robbed that stage or not? The idea was to lock the bastard up, Custis. If he hadn't pulled that job, we had him for four or five other heists for sure."

"I'm not arguing with that. But about two months before I picked Ortega up, wasn't there a train robbery near Red Horse?"

"Yeah. Now that you mention it, there was."

"How much was taken?"

"Enough gold to give the Wells Fargo executive I talked to a heart attack."

"Gold bars?"

"Freshly minted bullion. One hundred thousand dollars worth."

Longarm leaned back in his chair and cocked an eyebrow at Vail. "That's a lot of gold, all right."

"All right. Enough mystery. What in blazes are you drivin' at?"

Longarm lit up a fresh cheroot and related his adventures of the night before, including his perusal of a very interesting piece of anatomy. When he finished, Vail was shaking his head incredulously.

"I swear, Longarm, you draw pretty women to you the way a dead carcass draws flies."

Not particularly pleased at the way he'd put it, Longarm said, "I figure it should take at least a couple of weeks for me to track down that gold shipment. What I'm wondering, Vail—do you think Wells Fargo would be willing to give this here lady some kind of a reward?"

"No question."

"Good. Right now she thinks we're both going to get filthy rich. When it's all over, I'd like to be able to give her something for her help."

"You think she'll go along with that?"

"Depends. How much of a reward will Wells Fargo give her?"

"One percent."

"That'll make it one thousand then."

"If the gold bullion is all there."

"Then that'll have to satisfy her."

"What about those other three?"

"I'll deal with them when the time comes."

Longarm plucked his hat off Vail's desk and got to his feet.

"You leavin' today?" Vail asked.

"That's what I promised the lady."

"On your way out, see the clerk for your travel vouchers. I'll carry this as a follow-up to our investigation of the Wells Fargo train heist to make it easier for them idiots in Washington to understand."

"I'll take the afternoon train."

Leaning back in his swivel chair, Vail studied Longarm's face for a long moment, then winked. "Just don't spend all your time playing with that map."

"How else am I going to memorize it, Billy?"

Longarm clapped his hat on and left Vail's office.

He was only a block from his rooming house when he heard Consuela call his name softly from the mouth of an alley. He ducked into the alley. She had thrown a dark knitted shawl over her shoulders—but otherwise was dressed as she had been the night before.

Her eyes were wide with excitement.

"What's wrong, Consuela?"

"It's them! Haskins and Lars—and that other pig."

"Where are they?"

"Up in your room!" she hissed. "They wait for you now!"

"You sure?"

"I hear them downstairs when they ask the landlady for your room. So I hurry out of it. Before I go down the back stairs to alley, I see them push into your room. Then I wait down here for you to come."

"You sure they're still up there?"

"I am sure. I cross street further down until I can see your window. I see shadow standing in it, watching street. They are waiting for you to come."

"Persistent bastards."

"Now we go, hey?"

Without replying, Longarm left Consuela and walked back to the head of the alley and peered cautiously out. His rooming house was on this side, facing the street, the entrance set back from the sidewalk. From this angle he could not see the steps leading up to the door, nor the front of the rooming house. If he used the back entrance and charged up the stairs into his room, gun blazing, the furniture would get all chewed up. He'd probably shatter a window—and when it was all done, there'd likely be bloodstains on the wall. His long-suffering landlady would have a fit and do what she had been threatening to do ever since he took the room.

Kick him out.

Returning to Consuela, he took her arm and guided her deeper into the alley.

"Come on," he said. "We've got a train to catch."

Chapter 2

Longarm was the envy of every man on the train that brought him and Consuela to Red Horse. They arrived in the small mining town early in the evening, and as Longarm escorted Consuela from the train depot to the hotel, he noticed miners, roustabouts, and townsfolk halting in their tracks to get a better look at the provocatively sultry Mexican woman on Longarm's arm. The hotel desk clerk—a bald-pated, stove-up cowpoke—could only stare, his toothless mouth hanging open, as Longarm strode across the lobby with Consuela and halted at the front desk.

"Yes, sir?" the clerk managed.

"Two rooms for the night," Longarm told him.

"Two?"

"You heard me. Two."

Consuela dug Longarm in the ribs with her elbow. "Whatsa matter with you, gringo? You don' want to spend the night with Consuela?"

"That's right. I want to get some sleep."

"I let you sleep—later."

"You don't understand, Consuela. It wouldn't be seemly for us to sleep in the same room. We are not married, and besides, we are here on official business."

"Whatsa matter? Why you complain so much? We take one room, we save the government money."

Longarm was weakening. The desk clerk had been following the conversation closely and was beginning to salivate. It was obvious he was having trouble believing Longarm was really trying to talk Consuela out of sharing his room for the night.

"You know what I think?" Consuela said. "I think you afraid of Consuela. I am too much woman for you, huh?"

Longarm looked back at the clerk. "Make that one room."

"Yes, sir!" the clerk said.

He flipped the hotel register around and handed Longarm a pen. Longarm signed it, and the desk clerk hurried out from behind the front desk, snatched up Longarm's gear, and with astonishing alacrity led him and Consuela up the stairs. Entering the room ahead of them, he flung up the window with such enthusiasm he nearly catapulted himself out through it. Recovering nicely, he danced about and ran his hand over the bedspread, smoothing it down. As the old cowpoke backed out of the room, Longarm flipped him a coin. The door closed and Longarm turned to Consuela.

She was bouncing on the bed, her dark eyes gleaming.

"You like it?" he asked.

"Oh, yes. It is very good one. Hear that? No squeak."

"Well, you go ahead and bounce on it. I'm going downstairs to find the sheriff."

She made a face. "But Consuela is hungry!"

He shrugged. "All right. We'll go down now and eat supper downstairs in the hotel's dining room. I can see the sheriff afterward."

"You mean you go off and leave Consuela alone?"

"I won't be long," he assured her. "And you'll be safe enough if you stay up here in the room."

"All right. I come upstairs and wait for you." She smiled, her white teeth flashing in her dusky face. "When you come back, we try out this new bed."

Longarm sighed.

Sheriff Newland's deputy was leaning back in the sheriff's swivel chair, half asleep, when Longarm entered his office. The deputy was a lanky, rawboned fellow with crooked teeth, and judging from the vacant look in his pale blue eyes, air for brains. At Longarm's entrance, the deputy flipped up his hat brim to get a better look at him.

"You Sheriff Newland's deputy?" Longarm asked.

"Yep."

"Got any idea when Sheriff Newland will be back?"

"Nope."

"Where might he be?"

"He might be across the street in the Gold Nugget Saloon."

Longarm did not bother to thank the deputy as he left. Crossing back across the street, he pushed through the saloon's batwings and found it to be Red Horse's largest and gaudiest watering hole. As Longarm looked around its smoke-filled interior, he wished he'd had a nickel for every mining town that boasted a saloon called the Gold Nugget.

Sheriff Newland, his star gleaming on his vest, was playing poker at a table in the back with three other men. Unhappy men, judging from the neat pile of chips sitting in front of the sheriff. Newland glanced up as Longarm approached, then picked up the two cards dealt him, leaned back, and studied his hand, not a muscle on his craggy face moving, his eyes dead calm. Longarm figured the man to be in his early fifties. The betting began and when it was over, the sheriff proceeded to rake in another pile of chips.

"Like to speak to you, Sheriff," Longarm said softly. "When you can spare the time, that is."

"You in a hurry?"

"Not so you'd notice."

A sudden glint in his eyes, he glanced quickly around at the other players, then looked back up at Longarm.

"Well, now, mister," he drawled, "if I was you, I'd sure be in a hurry to get back to my hotel room with a filly like you just brung in waitin' for me."

The players at the sheriff's table broke into appreciative laughter. Longarm kept his composure. But it was not easy. He had already seen how much excitement a woman of Consuela's spectacular qualities could generate in this woman-starved mining town, and of course the desk clerk must have wasted no time spreading the word that he and Consuela were sharing a hotel room. So all in all, he could not really blame the sheriff for taking advantage of the opening Longarm had given him.

The laughter died down and the sheriff got to his feet.

"I'm out, gents," he told the players. "You'll have to get even some other time." He glanced over at Longarm. "I won't be long, mister."

Longarm waited for Newland to cash in his chips, and then the two of them crossed the street to his office. The deputy was asleep in Newland's chair, his feet still propped up onto the desk. Newland strode around behind the chair and spun it, nearly spilling the deputy onto the floor. The deputy jumped hastily to his feet, almost losing his hat in the process. With a mean grin on his face, Newland booted him enthusiastically in his rear end, sending the deputy windmilling out the door.

"Get off your ass, Earl," he called after the deputy. "Make your rounds."

Slumping down in his swivel chair, Newland motioned to a wooden chair beside his desk. "Sit down, Long. Sorry I couldn't meet you at the station. How was your trip?"

Longarm slumped down into the chair. "It was slow and hot."

"Usually is this time of year. How's Billy Vail these days?"

"Billy's doing just fine."

"Great lawman in his day. Yessir, he could track as good as any Apache and show them a few lessons in the bargain. As persistent as a summer cold and a helluva lot more deadly."

"He's put on a few pounds since then."

"Yeah. And I just get skinnier. Must be this damned heat. Your telegram didn't say much. What can I do for you?"

"I need some idea of the country around the town of Needle Gap."

"That's still hostile country."

"Indians?"

"Everything. Gunslicks. Mexicans. Renegade Utes, maybe even some Apaches. They're like ants in the woodwork. The Mexican banditos are the worst—stealing ore wagons. I guess they're doing their own crude smelting of the ore. Earl and I've gone after them a couple of times, but it's like chasing smoke. That's wild country, Long, fit only for brigands and murderers. I'm surprised you ain't heard about it."

"I heard about it. Only I was hoping I'd heard wrong. Well, then, first things first. I'll be needing a wagon."

"There's plenty for hire at the livery."

"I think I'll want something sturdier than that. High-backed. A small ore wagon maybe."

"Try the Colorado Mining yard on the other side of the train depot. They might have one they'll let you hire out. They don't use the little ones much anymore. With the veins giving out, they're hauling bigger chunks now. You want to tell me what you're after?"

"The Wells Fargo gold shipment that got heisted a while back."

"You mean you got a line on it?"

"I think so."

"How come you're taking this Mexican filly with you?"

"She's got the map."

"Why not take it from her and leave her behind."

"Can't. That's where it is."

"Huh?"

"On her behind. Tattooed."

"Jesus. You ain't kidding, are you?"

"I don't have that much imagination."

"You want my deputy to go along?"

"Nope. Too many cooks."

The sheriff nodded glumly. "Yeah. Besides, Earl wouldn't be much help, I'm thinkin'. Around here, he's not even good window dressing. How long you think it'll take?"

"Depends. If I don't run into trouble, I'll probably be back here in a week or two maybe."

Newland nodded. "Yeah, well, count on running into trouble. That's unfriendly country. So it might take a little longer."

"There's one more thing, Newland."

"What's that?"

"There might be three gents on my tail. The tall one's Lars Peterson. The next one is a fellow called Haskins. You won't have any trouble spotting Haskins. I stove in his face with his own blackjack. The third one's Amos, a little fat guy with mean eyes. He's a terrible poker player."

Newland laughed. "They shouldn't be hard to spot."

"Keep them occupied if you can."

"If they show up, I'll throw 'em in the lockup."

"On what charge?"

Newland grinned. "I'll think of something. I'll get Earl on it. Make the silly bastard earn his keep."

"Warn him to be careful. These men are a rum threesome, stupid but dangerous."

"The stupid ones always are."

"Thanks," Longarm said.

He got up, shook the sheriff's hand, and strode from the office.

Two days later, Earl spotted the three men Newland had warned him about swinging down off the train. Just as the sheriff had said, one of them had a bandage around his face. It covered his face so completely there was an opening for only one angry, bloodshot eye. Earl chuckled and followed the three as the shortest and fattest one was made to lug the others' gear as well as his own.

Earl kept well behind them as they crossed the tracks and headed for the hotel. Once they entered it, Earl sat on the bench in front of the barber shop and waited a while before following the three into the hotel. He asked the desk clerk which room the three men had taken, then went upstairs and knocked lightly on their door.

A furtive scuttling sound came from the other side of the door. He heard Lars Peterson's muffled voice close behind it. "Who is it?"

"Earl."

The door swung open and Earl strode in, a broad smile on his face. Lars slammed the door shut. Amos did a quick skip at sight of Earl. Lars shook his head, a big grin on his face. "Good to see you, boy."

Earl glanced across the room at Haskins, who had remained slumped onto the bed at Earl's entrance. He peered grouchily at Earl.

"You sure look awful, Hake," Earl told him.

"How the hell do you think I *feel*?" he demanded, his voice a guttural rasp, his mouth barely able to articulate his words.

"What the hell happened?"

"That sonofabitch Longarm. He did this to me and when I get my hands on him, he's going to die an Apache death, only slower."

"Well, I got some news'll make you feel better."

"Let's have it," said Lars.

"Yesterday, Long and Gasset's woman hired an ore wagon and left here on their way to pick up that gold shipment Ortega hid."

"Well, now, ain't that something," said Lars.

"You sure they're headin' for the gold?" Amos asked.

"What the hell do you think?" Earl shot at him. "Why else would they take that ore wagon?"

Lars glanced at Haskins. "What do you think, Hake? If they're using an ore wagon we won't have no trouble catchin' up to them. We'll have them in a couple of days."

"What's the all-fired hurry?" Hake grumbled. "Let the fools dig up the gold for us. Then we move in and take it."

"I don't like that, Hake," said Lars. "I say we kill the bastard, strip the girl naked, and study her backside. Then go after the gold ourselves. If we hang back, we might blow the whole thing."

"I ain't in no mood to argue," Haskins rasped.

Earl had never seen Hake this subdued. He was in too much pain even to argue with Lars.

"Go on," Haskins growled to them all. "Get out of here. Go downstairs and get soused if you want. I need some rest. This goddamn jaw is killing me."

Earl headed for the door. "Better let me go out first," he told the others. "Give me enough time to get across the street."

"You think this sheriff suspects who you are?"

Earl grinned. "Hell, no. He's the one sent me to the station to look out for you three. I'm supposed to tell him when you get in so he can lock you up."

"Lock us up? For what?"

"What I figure is he'll trump up some charge to keep you here—so you won't be no trouble for Longarm."

Lars chuckled. "Thanks for the warning. We'll be ready for him when he makes his move. Let him come."

"That suits me fine," said Earl. "I hate the bastard."

Earl slipped cautiously out of the room, then moved lightly down the stairs and out of the hotel.

Newland got quickly out of the barber's chair and walked over to the window to watch his deputy as he left the hotel. Once Earl passed out of his line of sight, he shifted his gaze to the hotel veranda.

"I ain't finished your shave, Sheriff," complained the barber. He was waiting behind the chair, his straight razor still flecked with lather.

"Hold it a minute, Wally," Newland said.

Two men left the hotel and paused on the porch. After a quick look around, they descended the porch steps and headed down the street in the direction of the Gold Nugget. Newland walked back to the barber chair and sat back down.

"Make it fast, Wally," he said, and leaned his head back onto the headrest.

The barber finished shaving him, peeled away the striped sheet, and snapped it. Newland got up, ran his palm over his chin, and paid the barber. He put his hat back on in the doorway and crossed the street to the hotel.

Old Pete was behind the desk. "Hi, Sheriff."

"Them two just left. What room?"

"Twenty-six, Sheriff."

"They alone?"

"There's another one still up there, I reckon. I don't blame him. He looked like he'd tangled with a grizzly."

"Thanks, Pete."

On the third floor, Newland advanced quietly down the hallway, found room number twenty-six, and knocked.

"Yeah?" The voice was barely audible.

"Sheriff Newland. Open up."

"Why should I?"

Newland heard the bed squeak. He kicked open the door. A big fellow, his head swathed in bandages, was standing by the bed in the act of lifting his sixgun out of his holster hung on the bedpost.

"Drop it, mister."

Slowly, the bandaged fellow lowered his gun. But he didn't drop it to the floor.

"Let it drop, I said."

The fellow opened his hand. The gun thumped heavily to the floor.

"Now, kick it over here."

The fellow kicked the sixgun, sending it spinning across the wooden floor toward him. And that was the last thing Newland remembered as someone brought the barrel of a sixgun down hard on the back of his skull.

Chapter 3

"Hold up," Longarm said, reaching forward and snaking his Winchester out of his scabbard.

Consuela, standing up in the front of the wagon bed, cursed and hauled back on the ribbons. The two powerful workhorses planted their massive hoofs and the ore wagon ground to a halt.

"Keep down," Longarm called as he spurred his horse across the trail and made for the base of the butte just ahead of them. Before he reached it, a rifle shot rang out from the butte's rim and the bullet whined off a rock face just behind him. Lowering his head, he kept on into the rocks at the base of the butte.

As soon as he was in cover, he glanced back at the wagon. The reins were still in Consuela's hand, but she had ducked down out of sight behind the wagon's high sides. Continuing on around the base of the butte, he came to a game trail leading to the rim. He booted the chestnut up it, and was close to the top of the butte when a second rifle shot nipped his hat brim. He leaped from his horse and dragged it under a rock ledge. After tethering it to a scrub pine, he continued his climb toward the rim on foot, his rifle at the ready. He didn't know how many men he was up against. He had caught the sunlight glinting off only one rifle barrel, but that didn't mean much. There could be a small army up there.

A shadow fell over Longarm. He flung himself about. A rifleman was standing on the rim between him and the sun, his sombrero riding on his back, his rifle tucked into his shoulder as he took aim. Longarm dove to the ground a second before the rifle cracked. The slug exploded into the ground inches from his left boot. Longarm swung up his rifle, sent a hurried round at the Mexican, then levering swiftly, sent a steady fusillade up at the exposed rifleman, who ducked hastily back off the rim.

Longarm ran on up the trail to the top of the butte, and saw that the Mexican had retreated to the rocks on its far rim, his sombrero visible above a boulder. Longarm flung himself prone, aimed carefully, and sent a round at the sombrero. The hat toppled out of sight. Longarm cranked and waited. But there was no return fire. Cautiously, he got to his feet and keeping low, ran a zigzag course across the top of the butte to the boulder. Reaching it, he peered over and saw the slumped body of the Mexican, his drilled sombrero on the ground beside him.

Longarm walked around the boulder, nudged the Mexican over onto his back, then bent over him. His last shot had left a crease along the top of the man's head, but that had not been the fatal slug. An earlier one had caught the man in the shoulder, and another shot had stamped a hole in his vest. The Mexican's string mustache drooped loosely over his open mouth and was not moving. Longarm leaned close and verified what he suspected. This Mexican would fire on no more gringos.

From below came Consuela's scream, followed by the sudden rumble of the ore wagon. He ran to the edge of the butte and saw a Mexican driving it off. He had snatched the reins from Consuela and was standing on the whiffletree as he guided the team. Three other Mexican riders were escorting the wagon as it rattled off down the trail. He could not see Consuela; he figured she was most likely still in the wagon, huddled down behind its high sides. In a moment the wagon was out of sight.

He left the dead Mexican for the vultures and ran back down the trail to his horse. By the time he had ridden around the base of the butte and gained the trail, he was able to see clearly ahead of him the plume of dust lifting into the air behind the wagon. He kept on after it, keeping the dust plume in sight but making no effort to overtake it. At dusk the plume vanished, but Longarm had no difficulty following the wagon's tracks after it turned off the trace, and by the time he came within sight of the Mexicans' campfire, it was just past dusk.

Dismounting a safe distance away, he tethered his horse in among some rocks and started for the camp, keeping first a huge boulder and then a clump of scrub pine between him and the campfire. Hunkering down inside the pine, he unholstered his .44 and peered through the branches. One of the Mexicans was bent over the campfire, holding a large iron skittle in the flames. Longarm could hear the jerky sizzling and could smell the beans and hot peppers he was frying with it.

Consuela was coiled on a blanket on the far side of the encampment, her back against a huge, flat-sided boulder. Two of the Mexicans were crowding close about her. Just beyond her in a small clearing was the ore wagon. The two workhorses and the Mexicans' mounts were in a rope corral farther away on the far side of the encampment, close by a stream.

The two Mexicans leaning over Consuela were obviously taunting her, commenting on the delights they would soon be sharing, no doubt. Their jackal-like laughter came dimly to Longarm. He looked away, his gaze searching the campsite for the fourth one. But he was nowhere in sight. Where the hell was he? Longarm looked back at Consuela, figuring the odds of freeing her from these banditos. He did not entirely like them. For one thing, if he were going to make a move on them, he would have to make damn sure they would not be able to snatch up Consuela and use her for a shield—or a hostage—forcing him either to lay down his weapon or clear out.

He pulled back from the pines, keeping an eye out for the missing Mexican, then darted around the campsite, keeping low, dodging from boulders to bush clumps. By the time he had reached a spot behind the boulder where Consuela was crouched, he still had not located the elusive bandito.

He cocked his .44 and considered his options.

By this time two of the Mexicans were squatting on a log beside the fire, finishing their supper. The third had brought a bowl of the jerky and peppers to Consuela and was hunkered down beside her, feeding himself noisily from the bowl. Occasionally, he would dart a sly glance at her, like a coyote sizing up a prairie dog just emerging from its den.

Suddenly one of the others by the fire called out to the bandito and held up a tequila jug. The conversation that followed was in Spanish, but Longarm knew enough of the language to know the one by the fire had told the Mexican with Consuela to come get it while he could, it was the last jug they had.

Heeding the call, the Mexican hastened down the slight slope to join his fellows. Soon he was bending the jug back with great enthusiasm, and as the three Mexicans passed the jug around, their hilarity grew with astonishing rapidity. Glancing continuously up at the full-breasted beauty they would soon be sharing, they slapped backs, dug each other in the ribs, and laughed in lusty anticipation of the feast ahead.

Crouching behind the boulder, Longarm watched them impatiently, waiting for the fourth Mexican to come and join the party.

But at last he realized he couldn't wait any longer.

"Consuela!" he whispered. "I'm over here, behind the rock!"

"Is that really you, Longarm?"

"Yes, dammit. Of course it is."

"Hah!" she whispered gleefully. "They say their man kill you!"

"Never mind that. Move over closer to me!"

"I can go nowhere, fool! They have tie my hands and feet."

"Damn," he muttered.

"So now what you do?" she demanded caustically. "Stay behind rock and watch them take me?"

Longarm holstered his gun and took out his pocket knife, opened it, and dropped onto his stomach. In plain sight of the drunken revelers around the campfire, he slithered across the ground, pushing his rifle ahead of him, until he was able to reach behind Consuela with his knife.

"Careful," she hissed as the cold blade brushed her wrist. "Do not cut me."

He sliced through the rawhide, then reached down and did the same to the rawhide binding her ankles.

"Who the hell are these banditos?" he asked, glancing nervously down the slope at them.

"They crazy." Consuela said, rubbing her hands together to restore circulation. "They see ore wagon, think we got plenty gold ore. That is what they do. They live in these hills and steal gold ore on way back to Needle Gap."

"Where's the other one? I counted four Mexicans when they rode off with the wagon."

"You mean Roberto. The others tell him to ride back, see what happen to that one who shoot at wagon."

"Then he'll be back soon. We'd better get the hell out of here while we can. Let's go."

"Wait!" she whispered. "I get my shoes."

As she reached for them, one of the banditos stood up suddenly to stare at her—and Longarm. Obviously, the darkness and his intoxication made it difficult for the Mexican to see Longarm's face clearly.

"Hey!" he cried. "Roberto?"

Without responding, Longarm folded his knife and pocketed it, then picked up his Winchester and cranked in a fresh round. The sound it made alerted the three. They snatched up their rifles and scrambled out of the campfire's light, scattering into the shadows. Longarm saw no sense in wasting a bullet on their shadowy figures. He took Consuela by the wrist and hauled her upright. For a moment she hung back in order to finish putting on her shoes, then scrambled after him as he plunged through the darkness toward the ore wagon.

When they reached it, he boosted Consuela up into it.

"Keep your head down," he told her. "Stay out of sight."

"Hey!" she cried, leaning over the side of the wagon. "Give me your knife!"

He tossed it up to her.

"Now, keep down!" he repeated.

Once she had obeyed, he headed back toward the campfire, making for a low clump of bushes that gave him a clear shot at the campsite still lit by the blazing fire. Pushing into the bushes, he lay flat and waited, his rifle on the ground in front of him, his finger hooked around the trigger. He figured the Mexicans would scout around, beat the bushes for a while, then return to their fire for its warmth, cursing the loss of their lush captive, their only recourse now being to finish that jug.

As he lay there, he heard them thrashing about in the bushes, running through the trees surrounding the campsite, occasionally shouting to one another—exhibiting, at best, a hapless confusion. They were unable to see clearly in the darkness, and in addition they were drunk half out of their minds. Listening to them floundering about, Longarm could not help but smile. They had expected an entirely different party than the one they were now attending.

At last a single Mexican straggled back to the campfire and reached for the jug. He was obviously too drunk to think clearly. Since he hadn't been fired upon, his tequila-fogged brain had foolishly decided Consuela and her rescuer had fled and posed no further threat. He was tipping up the jug when one of his companions stumbled out of the darkness to help him finish it. A moment later the third Mexican rejoined the party. Watching them cavort about the campfire, Longarm hesitated.

He knew that as soon as he and Consuela tried to hitch the wagon up, the three would be alerted and would take after them, drunk or not, which meant he really had no choice but to deal with them. With a sigh, he lifted his rifle and sighted on the jug just as one of the Mexicans was handing it to another. He squeezed the trigger. The jug exploded. The Mexicans flung themselves to the ground as the one holding the jug let out a cry and grabbed his right arm. Through the man's clenched fingers, blood spouted. A piece of the exploding jug must have sliced him.

"I got you cold," Longarm shouted to them. "I don't want to kill you. Drop your weapons. You're too drunk too fight."

"Hah, gringo," cried the tallest one, peering at the bushes where Longarm crouched, "we keel you, drunk or sober!"

As the Mexican swung up his rifle, Longarm squeezed off a shot. The Mexican buckled and dropped his weapon. Before the next one could get off a shot, Longarm cut him down as well, his slug catching him just above the belt buckle. The one with the bleeding arm flung himself to the ground and levering his rifle swiftly, sent a withering fusillade into the bushes. Longarm ducked low. Tiny bits of branches and twigs rained down upon him. Lifting his head slightly, he got off two more shots.

It was the second one that quieted the Mexican.

The silence that followed was awesome—as deafening as the gunfire had been. He crawled out of the bushes and moved carefully over to the downed Mexicans. There was enough light from the campfire for him to see that two of them had taken fatal wounds. The third was alive, but his chest wound looked pretty bad when Longarm peeled back his shirt.

The Mexican was still holding an ancient Navy Colt in his fist. Longarm gently disengaged the Colt from his grasp and flung it into the bushes.

The Mexican stirred and opened lidded, crafty eyes. "Hey, gringo, that's good weapon. Packs a wallop. Why you throw it away like that?"

"To keep you from using it on me."

"You crazy. I am already dead man."

"Maybe not."

"A man knows when he is going to die."

"Why'd you attack us?"

"We think you have gold ore in your wagon. Instead, it is empty. We make mistake. But we think, maybe the woman, she will warm our beds."

"She won't be warming your bed now."

"Anyway, we make good try."

"You were in no condition to fight. You should have dropped your rifles. I'm sorry this had to happen."

"Why you sorry, gringo? If we take your woman, we rape her. If we take you, we cut off your balls." He grinned, his teeth gleaming in his swarthy face.

"All that for gold."

"Gold is all that matters, gringo. Without it, life is one long constipation."

Reaching down, Longarm started to pull the Mexican's shirt out of his belt to get a better look at the wound. But the Mexican brushed his hand aside.

"I just want to get a better look at that wound," Longarm explained.

"Do not bother. I am going to do die. Are you priest?"

"No."

"You see how it is? Leave me be, gringo."

Longarm stood up. The Mexican seemed to relax. His eyes closed. Longarm stood over him, unwilling to let him die alone in the cold night. After a moment or two the Mexican's entire body seemed to shift and settle into the ground. Longarm turned and headed back to the wagon, cautiously now, on the lookout for Roberto, that other Mexican.

He was halfway to the wagon when he heard Consuela scream.

Digging hard, he ran back to the wagon. Before he reached it, Consuela stuck her head up over the wagon's side, a triumphant smile on her face.

"Hey! Come and see what I have done with your knife!"

Longarm put down his rifle and hauled himself up over the side of the wagon. Roberto was sprawled on the wagon's bed, the hilt of Longarm's knife sticking out of his side. He looked to be not much older than sixteen or seventeen. He stirred slightly, then groaned and opened his eyes, but when he tried to struggle to a sitting position, Longarm pushed him back down, then pulled out the knife. The kid gasped. A thin trickle of blood followed out after it, but the wound was obviously not fatal. No major arteries seemed to have been severed, and the pocket knife's blade was no more than a few inches long. He wiped off the knife on the Mexican's pants leg. Consuela reached down and took the knife from him.

"Looks like he'll live," Longarm told her, as he straightened. "That's not much of a wound."

"So then you finish him for me."

"You crazy? He's just a kid, looks like. Maybe we can save him."

"You are one crazy gringo! This one, he want to rape me."

"Well, he won't be so eager to rape anybody now."

"So now you can keel him."

He looked at her impatiently. "What the hell's the matter with you, Consuela? Why are you in such a hurry to kill this kid? Now keep him quiet while I see to the horses."

He jumped down to the ground, and was rounding the wagon when he heard what sounded like a struggle, followed by the wounded Mexican's sharp, strangled cry. Longarm turned around and clambered swiftly back up into the wagon. Consuela, Longarm's bloody pocket knife in her hand, was standing over the young Mexican. He was flat on his back now, a bloody ribbon under his chin where Consuela had slit his throat. From the slit, his dark blood had poured out onto the bed of the wagon. There was no doubt of it. He was dead.

Longarm looked incredulous at Consuela. "What happened?"

She shrugged, making no effort to show her indifference to his anger. "When you go, he jump up to take me. So I let heem get close, real close—and when he do, I slit his throat."

Longarm knew there was no way in the world that this wounded kid could have gotten up and made a grab for Consuela. He shook his head in wonderment at her casual duplicity. And then something else occurred to him.

"Consuela, how did this kid get up into this wagon in the first place?"

"I see him in the darkness. He has only revolver and is coming at you from behind, so I whisper down to him. He look up at me and I say for him to come up into the wagon, that I will give him a rifle."

"What else did you say you'd give him?"

She shrugged. "So . . . maybe I promise heem one more thing."

"Yeah, maybe you did."

"You angry with Consuela?"

"You just murdered a man in cold blood."

"Is that why you angry?"

"Yes."

"You are crazy. What is matter with you? You should be grateful to Consuela. She save your life." She smiled at him then, proudly. "Is that not true?"

"I suppose it is."

"Well, then!"

He looked at her for a long moment, her proud triumph still unsettling him. When the time came, it seemed, Consuela could do what had to be done. But what he could not understand was the pride she took in slitting that Mexican kid's throat. Men do terrible things and are eaten with remorse thereafter, but some women can do terrible things and be proud. Maybe that was the real difference between them.

Weary with thinking about it, Longarm grabbed the young Mexican by his belt and heaved him over the wagon's side, then jumped down after him and dragged him off into the brush. That done, he hurried off to hitch up the horses.

There was no way he was going to spend the night in this campsite. It had become a charnel house.

Chapter 4

As soon as Longarm harnessed the workhorses to the wagon, he took the hobbles from the Mexicans' mounts and fired his sixgun over the animals to send them on their way. In spite of Consuela's protests, Longarm did not return to the trace, but cut directly into the badlands and kept going until sometime after midnight, when they made a dry camp on a rocky tableland.

It was a sullen, naked Consuela who eventually slumped down beside him and waited for him to open his soogan so she could join him. When he did not open it for her, she sat back on her haunches, pouting.

"What is the matter, Custees?"

"I'm too tired."

"That's so? You sure it is not something else?"

"I'm tired, Consuela. You have your own blanket."

"It ees not enough. You are warmer than such a

blanket. Besides, Consuela does not like to sleep alone when she do not have to."

"Tonight you have to."

"You are no gentleman, I think."

Longarm reached over for his hat, put it on, grabbed his britches and boots, and stood up.

"Sleep under my soogan, then," he told her. "Where did you leave your blanket?"

"It ees by the wagon."

He started after it.

"Consuela is too much woman for the gringo!" she called after him.

He didn't bother to respond. He found her blanket rolled up near the wagon's rear wheel, gathered it up, and took it to a spot well above the wagon, one that gave him a clear view of the campsite—and of Consuela making herself comfortable under his soogan. He thought he could hear her peeved grumbling even at this distance. He closed his eyes and was asleep almost at once.

At dawn he came awake to the sharp aroma of fresh coffee. He glanced down at the campsite and saw Consuela busy over a crackling campfire. The coffee's aroma mingled with that of beans and bacon frying in the pan, its savory smell enough to pull him swiftly upright. He grabbed his hat and pulled on his pants, then called down a greeting to Consuela.

Seemingly less upset than the night before, she turned and waved to him.

When he got to the campsite, he asked, "Where'd you get the water for the coffee?"

She pointed down a gully. "When I wake up, I see the tops of willows down there. I go down and find small stream. The water, it run clear and fast. I take bath while you sleep, lazyhead."

"Guess I'll do the same," he said, heading over to where his soogan was to get his straight razor.

He was naked, shaving in icy-cold water up to his waist, when Consuela appeared on the bank beside him.

"Breakfast, she is ready."

"I'll be right out," he told her, scraping the whiskers off his chin. The cold water was not making it any easier for him.

She watched him as he finished shaving. Then, when he folded the razor shut and tossed it onto the bank alongside his clothing, she smiled at him seductively—no trace of the previous evening's anger in her eyes.

"If you want," she said, "I will help you dress."

"Won't the coffee get cold?"

"Oh, no. I can heat it up."

"My stomach is rumbling. Besides, we got a long ways to go yet, Consuela."

Her smile vanished. "What is the matter? You no like Consuela anymore?"

"Don't be silly," he said.

He ducked his head under the surface and swam a ways underwater. When he surfaced, he looked back and saw Consuela on her way back to the camp. From her angry, hip-swiveling stride, he was able to gauge her considerable fury. He sighed. A woman scorned could be a problem, and there was no sense in multiplying his problems by refusing to service this hot-blooded wench the next time she presented herself to him.

When he returned to the encampment, much invigorated by his swim and ready to eat a horse, he found

43

Consuela had calmed down some. Perhaps she'd figured it wasn't always a good idea to taunt Longarm about his manhood. She was obviously wondering what had cooled Longarm's ardor—but he had no intention of reminding her of that young Mexican's death. Meanwhile, he found the breakfast delicious, her coffee—as usual—as bracing and as strong as a smithy's right arm.

Later, swinging up into his saddle, he turned his mount and watched Consuela climbing into the wagon, the ribbons held in her left hand.

"Follow me as close as you can," he told her. "But I'll have to scout ahead for the best trail. If you lose me, don't tire the horses, just pull up and wait."

Standing up in the wagon, she shook her head. "This ees not so good, Custees."

"Why?"

"How you know which way you go? You not look at me for long time."

He grinned up at her. "I'll be taking another look at your lovely ass as soon as I can spare the time. Until then we'll just head due west until we hit that river I saw on your backside. Then we'll follow it north to Needle Gap."

"Consuela can hardly wait," she grumbled, flicking the reins.

The ore wagon groaned forward. Clapping spurs to his horse, Longarm rode on past the wagon.

Sheriff Newland awakened from a disordered sleep to find himself in Doc Winner's office over the saloon. The piano below him was tinkling away at a great rate, the sound of tramping feet and boisterous male voices coming through the floor with relentless clarity. He lifted his head. A lighted lamp sat on a table by the window. The raucous pounding of the miners' boots on the saloon's wooden floor below continued to pulse through his bed. Judging from the vigor of the miners' pounding, it was not very late.

He flung aside his blanket and sat up. Too quickly. Pain rocketed through his skull, bad enough to make his teeth ache. He hung on to the bed, sitting still, waiting for the pain to subside. Gradually it eased, and after relieving himself in the chamber pot, he sat back down on the bed and reached up to his head to feel the heavy bandage the doc had wrapped around it. He knew who had clubbed him—his sonofabitchin' deputy. There was no doubt in his mind. Just a second before the gun barrel came down, he had smelled the bay rum hair oil Earl favored—that and his lizard-guts breath.

The door opened and the doc entered.

He was a towering, hearty man with an indestructible constitution, judging from the fact that he rarely slept yet was never tired, drank like an Indian and was never drunk. At the moment he held a nearly full stein of beer in his hand, the suds creeping down its side. When he saw Newland sitting woozily on the edge of the bed, his beefy face broke into a wide grin.

"Had a hunch," he said, walking over to the bed. "Thought that noise downstairs would rouse you. Here, I brought you something to calm your senses and ease your bones."

He handed the stein to Newland, who took it gratefully in both his hands. He dipped his head back and downed its contents in a series of eager gulps.

"Thanks," Newland said, handing back the stein. "That sure as hell hit the spot."

"Best medicine in the world," said the doc. "Now, do you think that bandage is strong enough to keep your thick skull in one piece?"

"Seems to be doin' the trick, Doc. How bad am I hurt?"

"You're lucky. I'd say you was born with a pretty thick skull. It wasn't cracked open, mind you. But there's quite a lump there, so I figure you've got yourself a concussion, and that's not something I'd take lightly, if I were you."

"Then you figure I can ride out of here."

"No reason why not."

"How long have I been unconscious?"

"A day and a half."

"Son of a bitch. That means the bastard's got a good head start."

"And just who might that bastard be?"

"Earl."

"Your deputy?"

"You know any other Earls in this town?"

"I was just surprised is all. But why in hell would Earl want to clobber you? Ain't you been treatin' him right?"

"That ain't it. I sent him to keep a lookout for three men, and from the look of it, he joined up with them."

"How come?"

Newland looked wearily at the doc. "Gold, Doc. Gold."

"Gold?"

"Gold bullion Ortega Gasset's hid away somewhere, and he's after it."

"Ah, yes. The dream of riches. Ali Baba's cave. It's what makes the world go round, all right."

"How late is it, Doc?"

The doctor consulted his gold watch. "Seven-thirty. The evenin's young."

"Good. I need some food and a bath. Then I'll be ridin' out."

"You mean leave Red Horse without a sheriff to keep order."

"The town constable can spell me while I'm gone. I aim to bring back Earl—or his remains."

"You do sound determined."

Newland stood up. "How much do I owe you, Doc?"

The big man ran his hand over his chin. "Well, I wasn't going to petition you for the debt so soon, Sheriff, but I guess maybe I better get it now—while I still can, hey?"

"How much? I got to get a move on."

"Five dollars—counting the beer."

Newland dug into his Levi's side pocket and handed the doc his fee in silver coins, then strode on past him out the door.

From the landing above him, the doc called, "Keep your ass down, Sheriff."

Newland pushed out the side entrance and onto the sidewalk. He hoped he could keep going without passing out. At the moment he wasn't sure if it was his head which hurt the most or his empty stomach.

It was Earl who first spotted the buzzards. Calling out to

Lars, he pointed to them. "Looks like there's been some trouble ahead."

Squinting into the glare of the cloudless sky, Lars nodded. "That's what it looks like."

Amos glanced nervously over his shoulder. "Think maybe we ought to get off this trail? We're sure exposed."

"Cut your whinin'," Haskins snarled. "We got to follow these wheel tracks."

Haskins had been in a miserable mood since leaving Red Horse, and nothing anyone could say or do could shake him out of it. Earl realized the man was in no condition for this kind of hard riding. He was amazed the son of a bitch had gotten this far with half his face stove in. He was still their leader, of course, but Lars was beginning to act more and more without consulting Haskins, and Haskins didn't seem to mind.

"Maybe we could go up in the rocks," Amos suggested nervously. "Get ourselves above this trace."

"Whatsamatter, Amos?" Earl said, grinning at him. "Ain't you got the stomach for this?"

"Hell, yes, I have."

"Hell, no. You're as yellow as a jar of mustard."

"We can't go up into those rocks, Amos," Lars told him, showing more patience than the others. "That would tire the horses too much. And Hake ain't in no condition for that kind of riding."

"That's right," said Haskins, as he pulled his horse alongside Amos. "So we're staying right here on this trace."

"Hey, sure," said Amos hastily. "I was just makin' a suggestion."

"Keep your suggestions to yourself," Haskins growled, his one visible eye regarding Amos malevolently. "Whatever you say ain't worth a pinch of coon shit anyway."

Thoroughly chastened, Amos turned away from Haskins and booted his mount to a lope so as to distance himself from Haskins's mean gaze. The rest made no effort to keep up with him, content to let him ride point, pleased to be rid of his whining.

And that was just fine with Amos. Anything to be free of Haskins's snarling disapproval. Not that the others were any better. In fact, all of them treated him like a slave, and he was damned sick and tired of it. Trouble was, he saw no way out. He couldn't live in this wild land alone. He had to have such men around him to protect him from others who were even more ruthless.

Close to the spot where the buzzards were coming to earth, he dismounted, pulled his rifle from its sling, and left the trace to investigate on foot. As he moved deeper into the trackless badlands, he had to force himself to keep going, but he did, determined to show them back there that he wasn't yellow. A quarter of a mile into the badlands, he stepped softly around a canyon wall and saw an Indian picking over a corpse, a flock of unhappy buzzards waddling around him, fluttering their wings in protest. Another Indian was coming down from the rocks some distance away. At Amos's sudden appearance, the closest Indian stood up quickly and raised his hand in greeting.

In a fever of anxiety, Amos flung up his rifle and fired. He was lucky. Despite his trembling hands, the round found its mark. The Indian fell forward over the corpse, his hat falling off his head. Amos swung the rifle around to catch the second Indian in his sights, but the redskin had already vanished back up into the rocks.

Lars was the first to reach Amos. He had caught up the reins of Amos's mount out on the trace and had brought it along with him. Meanwhile, Amos had backed up and sat down on a flat boulder, sweat pouring down his face as he peered across the flat at the dead Indian. Lars released Amos's horse, rode on past him, then circled what had apparently been a campsite. He stayed on his horse as he inspected the three dead Mexicans, noted the Indian Amos had shot still draped over one dead Mexican, then rode back to Amos.

"Looks like you killed yourself an Indian," Lars said, reining up beside him.

"Yeah. That's right. I killed the bastard. He was robbin' them dead greasers."

Amos looked eagerly up at Lars. He could hear the others galloping up to join them and was looking forward to their approval, their hearty, booming laughter, their back-slapping congratulations. They wouldn't be calling him yellow now.

"Was that redskin the only one?" Lars asked.

"There was another one. Soon's I opened up, he made tracks, back up into them rocks over there."

Earl and Haskins clattered up and pulled their horses to a halt, staring beyond Amos and Lars to the buzzards feeding on the three Mexican corpses and the dead Indian draped over the nearest one. Their eyes were troubled. There was no hearty laughter or congratulations, nothing. It was not going the way Amos had thought it would.

"There's three dead Mex's out there," Lars told

Haskins and Earl. "And one dead Ute, looks like. Amos said the redskin was robbin' the corpses when he popped him."

"Move in," said Earl. "Let's take a better look."

Amos slipped his rifle back into his saddle sling, climbed aboard his horse, and followed the others. When they reached the dead Indian, they found he was still clutching a gold pocket watch he had taken from the Mexican. He was a Ute, which was what they had already surmised. His black Stetson had an eagle feather stuck in its band and lay on its side about a foot from the dead Mex. An ancient Navy Colt was stuck in the Ute's belt.

Earl reached down and took the Colt. The action was enough to dislodge the Ute from the corpse. His hand still frozen about the gold watch, he slipped sideways off the dead Mexican and landed face up. Earl let loose a gob of tobacco and hit the dead Indian's forehead. Then he looked more closely at the dead Mexican. It was an unsettling sight. No flesh was left on the dead man's face and his eye sockets were as deep and as hollow as death.

Haskins got down from his horse, peered closely at the dead Ute, then kicked him in the head so hard his face spun around and slammed into the ground. Then he glared up at Amos.

"This redskin's good and dead, all right, you damn fool," he muttered. "Now we got to watch out for Utes."

"Yeah, Amos," said Earl. "Maybe you should've held your fire."

"Hey," cried Amos. "I thought the Ute killed the Mex and was robbin' him."

"That what you thought?"

"Yeah . . . sure it was."

The others were grinning at him now. Like he was a kid got his hand caught in a cookie jar.

"Well, you was wrong, you stupid shit."

"Leave Amos alone," said Lars. "One thing's for sure. The Ute *was* robbin' this dead greaser."

Earl was glancing nervously around at the campsite. After a moment he shook his head. "Jesus. Lookit all these dead greasers. There sure as hell was a massacre here, all right."

"Maybe the Utes did it!" suggested Amos, desperate to redeem himself in their eyes for having shot the Ute.

"These greasers've been dead for days, you stupid asshole," said Earl. "That Ute just got here. He was only following the vultures—like you."

"Hold it," said Lars. "I think I see something over there."

He dismounted and walked past two of the dead Mexicans, then kept on, his eyes on the ground. After a moment he paused and beckoned to them. "Come over here and look at this!"

Earl and Haskins dismounted and joined him, Amos bringing up the rear. They all saw at once what he had discovered.

"Tire tracks," Earl said. "And them tires're cuttin' deep."

"An ore wagon," said Lars. "Sure enough."

"Now it makes sense," Haskins grated, his voice still painful to hear. "That bastard Longarm's the one left these dead greasers. He was fighting them off."

"This must be the same gang been robbing the ore wagons," Earl said. "Newland and I knew they was out here, but we never could track them. Looks like we won't need to track them now, the poor bastards."

"Which way's the wagon headin'?" Haskins asked.

Leaving them, Lars followed the tracks for about twenty yards, then held up and turned.

"They're headin' due west!"

As Lars walked back to them, Amos piped up hopefully, "Jesus. We maybe wouldn't've found them tracks if I hadn't left the trace to check on these buzzards."

"I s'pose," said Earl grudgingly.

"Guess we're lucky at that," said Lars, slapping Amos on the back.

Haskins would have none of it. He grunted something unpleasant under his breath and lifted his head to gaze about him at the high cliffs towering over them.

"Well, one thing's for sure," he grumbled. "We won't *stay* lucky if we hang around here—not with them Utes up there in the rocks."

"But I only saw one," Amos told him.

"What the hell's that supposed to mean, you damn fool? You willin' to guarantee there's only one more Ute up there?"

They walked back to their horses. Haskins grabbed his saddlehorn and, wincing in pain, hauled himself up into his saddle. Lars and Earl mounted up also.

Amos was just grabbing his saddlehorn when something powerful slammed into his back just below the back of his head, shattering his spine. He was dead so quickly he did not hear the rifle's crack. His right hand slipped from the saddlehorn and he fell backward to the ground without uttering a sound.

Haskins looked down at Amos's sprawled form and for the first time since leaving Denver, he raised his voice:

"Ride, boys, ride! Amos is a dead man."

They needed no urging. As they followed the ore wagon's tracks across the flat, then clattered over a gravelly wash, two more rifle shots rang out from the rocks above. Out of range by then, the men kept on without a single glance back. The pound of their hooves faded, leaving Amos to stare sightlessly up at the brutal sun, the only respite from its glare the occasional fleeting shadows cast by the descending buzzards.

Dan Two Feather emerged from the rocks, Billy Indian and Joe Big Hat behind him. Their faces were round and squat, their eyes like black raisins set in narrow cracks, their hooked noses like granite outcroppings. They were dressed in a motley of Indian and Western finery. All three wore Stetsons, with two of them boasting a single eagle feather stuck in the hatband. The sleeves on their cotton shirts had been cut off at the shoulders, and the seats of their Levi's had been cut out to make room for their breechclouts. Billy Indian and Joe Big Hat wore leather vests decorated gaudily with silver conchos and bronze bullet casings. Holstered sixguns hung from their gunbelts, and each one carried a Winchester.

They crossed the ground to where Long Bird lay sprawled beside the dead Mexican. Brushing back the feeding birds with the barrel of his Winchester, Dan Two Feather bent over Long Bird and brushed off the gob of tobacco juice remaining on his forehead. Slowly but firmly, he bent back each of the fingers on Long Bird's right hand until he had wrested the gold watch from his dead grasp. Then he stood up and held out the gold watch and chain to Billy Indian.

"He was your brother," said Dan Two Feather, speaking in their Ute tongue. "You take it."

Billy Indian took the watch and hefted it, then snapped open the cover protecting its face. He studied it for a moment, then held it up to his ear to listen to its steady tick.

"It is gold. But it is not worth the life of Long Bird."

Billy Indian walked over to the dead white eyes he had shot from the rocks. When he reached him, he unsheathed his knife, circled the white eye's scalp lock with the tip of his knife, then snapped off the bloody trophy and tucked it into his belt.

"We bury Long Bird," Billy Indian said. "Then we go after the other white eyes."

"Why?" asked Dan Two Feather. "You have already killed the one who shot Long Bird. And it is no longer allowed that an Indian can take a white eyes' scalp."

"Does Geronimo know this?" Joe Big Hat asked.

"Then I will go after the white eyes alone," said Billy Indian. "Did you not see what they did?"

"I saw."

"They did not care that our brother had been murdered. They were pleased. They kicked his body. One of them spat on him."

"Yes, I saw this," said Joe Big Hat.

"And I saw it too," admitted Dan Two Feather.

"Well, then?"

"I think you want excuse to kill more white eyes."

55

Billy Indian's smile was brilliant. "You are as wise as the eagle and fly as far as the hawk. You know as I do that any excuse to kill a white man is a good excuse."

Joe Big Hat said, "The only good white man is a dead white man."

"Brother," said Billy Indian, suppressing a chuckle, "you speak my thoughts completely."

"First, we will bury our brother and sing over his grave," said Dan Two Feather. "Then we will go after the three white eyes."

Billy Indian and Joe Big Hat lifted Long Bird's body between them and, with Dan Two Feather leading the way, carried him back toward the rocks. In a moment they had disappeared up the steep trail. They would bury their brother high in the rocks, safe from the coyote and the wolf.

Chapter 5

"You finished yet?" Consuela asked. "I'm getting cold."

"Hold on," Longarm told her. "Just a few minutes more."

There was little light left in the sky, and the swift mountain stream plunging through the chasm far below them filled the night with its soothing, rushing sound. Longarm had been studying Consuela's map for at least five minutes, but he was having difficulty reading that portion of Consuela's buns showing the region north and west of Needle Rock.

As he recalled, the town was surrounded by bluffs and young, sheer mountains. He'd been to the town before. It was a ghost of a former mining town that attracted gunslicks and other assorted outlaws on the run. But he knew little of the country beyond it, and there was not much to help him on Consuela's backside, except for two small, bracketlike half-moons north and west of the town indicating canyons. According to the map, Ortega had cached the gold in the second canyon, at the base of its southern wall.

Sitting back on his haunches, Longarm slapped Consuela's ass smartly to indicate he was done.

"Ouch!" she cried, rolling quickly over to face him.

"Thought you'd gone asleep."

"You devil!"

Gazing at her lush, naked figure, Longarm found in his own heart no trace of that reluctance that had kept her out from under his soogan these past three nights. Perhaps her ruthless disposal of that young Mex had become part of her charm; it meant he was dealing with a formidable wildcat who went her own way without looking back. She was a good deal tougher than she had let on back in Denver—and it was time he accepted that fact.

At the moment her dark eyes gleamed with a sultry, seductive glow, and there was a wicked smile on her full, pouting lips. His gaze swept her long, graceful neck, noted the bold thrust of her shoulders, the lush swell of her ripe, melonlike breasts. Watching him, she stirred slightly, just enough to open her thighs to him, revealing her gleaming coil of pubic hair, lush tendrils of which reached clear to her navel. Her white teeth flashed in her dusky face.

"What maps do you see on me now, Custees?"

"Doesn't have anything to do with gold," he admitted.

Without further ado, he slipped out of his pants and joined Consuela on the blanket. As he bore her down under him, her arms twined sinuously about his neck.

With a sigh she accepted his quick penetration and engulfed his erection in her hot, silken muff. Grunting eagerly, she shifted swiftly under him, rocked back, and swung up her legs, scissoring his waist.

"Don't cut me in half," he gasped.

"Shut up and fuck me, gringo!"

They went at it then with a wild frenzy, slamming at each other, grunting, crying out, grim-faced with intensity. They were like two wild animals clawing over a piece of raw meat as their lovemaking rose to a towering crescendo until Consuela's echoing shriek punctuated her shuddering orgasm. Close to the crest himself, Longarm heard her call out, and as she trembled wildly under him, went over the edge himself.

"No more," he muttered, dropping limply off her, her exultant cry still echoing in the rocks about them.

"All right, Custees," she said, moving sinuously up onto him and resting her cheek on his chest's thick, wiry nap of hair. "No more. Not for right now, anyway."

Gleaming beads of perspiration covered her arms and shoulders. She moved up onto his prone body and kissed him on the lips, thrusting her tongue deep into his mouth, probing wantonly. Then she pulled back and kissed him on the eyelids.

"You ready for some more now?" she asked sweetly.

"I'm done, Consuela. At least for now."

Her hand dropped onto his crotch. He laughed at the disappointment and scorn he saw in her eyes.

"I tell you what," he told her. "Next time find a bull buffalo. I understand they never give up."

"Maybe I can fix it for you."

"You mean fix it for *you*. Wake me up when I'm ready."

She slapped him smartly on his stomach.

"Ouch," he sad, laughing.

"Well, well, well," said an amused voice close behind them.

Longarm snapped his head around as Lars Peterson stepped out of a clump of scrub pine, his sixgun leveled on him. Haskins—his head and half of his face wrapped in a bandage—was close behind him, and after him came the Red Horse deputy. They had left the small fat one behind, apparently.

"You two sure make a lot of noise," said Peterson.

"We just got here," said the deputy. "Go ahead. Don't let us stop you."

Lars Peterson examined Consuela with undisguised lust, then glanced at Longarm.

"Too bad you couldn't satisfy the lady, lawman. We'll just have to see what we can do to help her out."

Consuela sat up and spat in his face. "Maggots like you can not satisfy a woman," she hissed.

"Yeah?" said Earl. "How come you're givin' yourself airs? You're only a dance-hall whore."

He grabbed Consuela's wrist and yanked her upright.

"Cut that out, Earl," said Haskins, his voice coming not too clearly through his bandage. "We don't want to do nothin' to hurt that pretty little map."

"Get up," Peterson told Longarm.

Pulling on his pants, Longarm got to his feet and stepped hastily into his boots.

"Now turn around."

Longarm turned and Peterson clubbed his lights out so fast, he didn't remember hitting the ground.

When he came to, it was daylight and he was sitting up on the ground with the back of his pounding head against the ore wagon's front wheel, his hands bound behind him with rawhide. His head still rang from the blow that had brought him down. Consuela was crouched close beside him. They had let her put on her blouse, but nothing more. Her skirt was sprawled on the ground in front of her. He could tell from her sullen, angry glare as she regarded the three men that, where they were concerned, they had not wasted the night.

The deputy was standing guard over them, and when he saw Longarm's eyes come open, he walked over to tell the others, who were peering off the cliff at the stream below. As soon as Earl left them, Consuela reached under her skirt for Longarm's knife, leaned over, and slashed at Longarm's rawhide bonds. She was in too much of a hurry to be careful, and in her haste sliced into his wrists, the blood flowing swiftly. She sliced again, this time severing a few of the rawhide strands. Then, leaving the knife in his hand, she straightened up just a second before the three men turned and started back to them.

Grinning like jackals approaching a dead carcass, the three men pulled up to stare down at Longarm.

"Yep," said Earl. "The bastard's come around."

"Now we can kill the sonofabitch," said Lars. "Slowly."

"And you can watch it all, bitch," Haskins said to Consuela, his one visible eye alight with anticipation.

"You men are crazy," she snapped.

Haskins shrugged. "Gold makes strange bedfellows at that. But right now this lawman is goin' to pay for what he done to me. And he can thank you for getting him into this."

"You gents talk a nice game," said Longarm. "Why don't you get on with it."

As he spoke he eased his blood-slicked wrists free of the rawhide still binding them and closed his right hand about his knife's handle. Haskins stepped forward and kicked Longarm in the side, the tip of his boot digging deep. The pain was fearful, but not unbearable, and Longarm kept himself upright. Then Lars Peterson joined the party, aiming a kick at Longarm's face. This time, Longarm ducked aside, reached up with his bloody left hand, and grabbed the man's boot. Twisting violently, he sent Lars plunging to the ground. Jumping up then, Longarm kicked Haskins in the stomach. Haskins doubled up and collapsed forward onto the ground, gasping for breath. Earl stepped back and drew his sixgun. Longarm put his head down and slammed into him, driving him violently backward. But Lars had already regained his feet and pounced on Longarm from behind.

Longarm lashed out with his knife and drove him momentarily back, then raced to the edge of the cliff. The stream below was a swift one, white water showing for the most part, and there were boulders close in under the canyon rim, the water foaming and swirling about them. Behind him, Longarm heard the three coming after him.

He had no choice.

Feet first, he stepped out into space.

• • •

It couldn't have been long, but his plunge seemed to last forever. Keeping himself from slanting over, he knifed feet first into the stream and, a second later, struck bottom, his boots digging into the sandy streambed. He tucked his knife into his right boot, then fought his way to the surface. But even as his head bobbed out of the frigid water, the shallow mountain stream's powerful current caught him up and swept him downstream with such irresistible force he could neither strike out for the stream bank, nor grab hold of any boulders to help slacken his pace. Like any other piece of flotsam caught in its impetuous flow, he was swept relentlessly along.

Rushing toward a bend in the stream, he saw ahead of him a huge boulder imbedded solidly in the streambed. Twisting his body around just in time, he managed to slam against it sideways. Like a swatted fly, he remained flattened on the boulder's broad surface. Digging his feet into the gravelly streambed at the boulder's base, he thrust his head and shoulders out of the water.

As he sucked air into his lungs, rifle fire erupted from the rocks above. The slugs came close enough to chip solid chunks off the boulder and send geysers of water into the air all about him. Above the rattle of the three men's gunfire, he could hear their derisive shouts. They sounded like carnival revelers in a shooting gallery.

A round passed within inches of his skull, slamming into the boulder's flank. Shards of stone dug into the side of his head. He took one last deep breath and, ducking under the water, swam toward the stream bank. Though he kicked his long legs powerfully, he was unable to make headway against the current, and it swept him farther downstream into a narrow passageway between a boulder and a submerged rock shelf projecting out from the stream's bank.

Twisting about so that his shoulders were caught between the boulder and the rock shelf, he managed to plant his feet solidly into the streambed under him. He lifted his head once more above the surface and found a sheer wall of rock looming between him and the rim high above, shielding him from his well-wishers. If he remained where he was, he would be safe—at least for now. But nothing need prevent them from descending to the stream to finish him off. Soon they would be racing up and down both sides of the steam, taking potshots at him, betting on whose bullet would finish him first.

He grabbed the rock shelf and pulled himself out of the water and up onto the stream's bank. He lay on his side for a while, sopping wet, as heavy and as frigid as a beached whale. He felt as if he had been through a millrace without missing a single paddle. A deep, obliterating weariness fell over him. He tried to keep his eyes open but it was impossible; the last thing he remembered was the long reach of the canyon wall bending over him and the high, cloudless blue sky above.

He awoke in a sweat. How long had he been lying on this rock slab? He glanced up at the sky, and saw it was still daylight. He pulled off his boots and emptied the icy water from them, then rubbed his feet and ankles until he felt the blood flowing back into them. Once the circulation had been restored, he pulled his boots back on, slipped the knife back into his right boot, then pushed himself erect and moved swiftly along the rock ledge, keeping close to the cliff face until he gained a clear view of the canyon's rim high above him. He saw no sign of Haskins and the others. But that didn't mean a thing, he knew. They were probably already on their way down here to finish him off.

He kept going and about fifty feet farther on, he came to a gravelly wash that split the canyon wall. He saw at once that this might be a way for him to make it back up to the canyon's rim. He started up the wash, and had gone about a hundred yards when he came to a spot where a portion of the rock wall had been gouged out by centuries of water pounding down the gully and slamming into it, before churning down to the stream below.

Longarm decided to take this opportunity to rest up and dry out some. His pants still clung to him, chilling him clear to his bone marrow. He pulled them off and moved deeper into the cavern, hunkered down, and leaned back against the rock—his eyes on the bright world beyond the cavern's mouth. In the next half hour a jackrabbit hopped past the cavern's entrance, and not long after, an antelope came into view. It was a yearling, its great soulful eyes peering for a moment into the cavern as it picked its way swiftly, delicately down the wash to the stream below. Then, from somewhere above, a flock of blackbirds raised a sudden, raucous clamor. Judging from the amount of noise they made, they were very much annoyed. Someone or something was on the trail below them. As they flew off, their angry outcry faded, and afterward, a deep, impenetrable silence fell over the canyon—as if every living creature in the canyon was watching and waiting.

Longarm pulled on his still-damp pants and waited too.

Time was measured by the slow movement of shadows across the rocks beyond the cavern's mouth. And still Longarm waited. Abruptly, he heard the clink of shod hoofs on stone coming from the wash above. Holding his knife in his right hand, he picked his way silently to the mouth of the cavern. The clang of iron on stone came almost constantly now, and with it the squeak of saddle leather, the jingle of bits. Occasionally a shod hoof sent polished stones rolling down the wash ahead of it.

Voices came then, barely intelligible at first.

Longarm got to his feet and flattened himself against the cavern's inside wall so anyone glancing in would not see him.

The first rider to pass was Lars Peterson, his tall, gangling figure leaning back in the saddle to make it easy on his mount. Behind him came the deputy, and then Haskins aboard a powerful dapple gray. Haskins had unwound the bandage covering his head so that it now hung loosely about his neck and shoulders like an oversized neckerchief. There was no sign of Consuela. He imagined she was somewhere back up on the canyon rim, trussed securely and probably flung into the ore wagon for safekeeping.

Longarm emerged from the cavern in a low crouch and in three quick strides overtook Haskins's horse. Laying a hand on the horse's rump, he boosted himself up onto the cantle. At the same time he flung his left arm around Haskins's neck, drew his head back, and with his right hand held his knife blade against Haskins's taut neck.

"You ready for a shave, Haskins?" Longarm whispered.

"What in . . . !"

Longarm leaned close. "Cry out and you're a dead man. Drop off your horse."

Instead, Haskins let out a bellow and went for his gun. At the same time, in a frantic effort to get loose, he plunged his head forward. Longarm felt the blade slice into Haskins's throat and heard the man's sharp cry of terror a second before his jugular was severed. Ahead of him, Earl and Lars Peterson wheeled their horses. Unbuckling Haskins's gunbelt, he clapped it about his waist, drew it tight, shoved Haskins off the horse, then turned the dapple gray around and spurred it back up the wash.

As Lars and Earl fired at him, he turned in the saddle and sent a shot back at them. Earl's horse went down with a squeal, catapulting Earl over its head. By then the gray was pulling Longarm out of sight around a rock wall. Bending low over it, he urged the horse on. Scrambling at times, but never faltering, the powerful animal performed magnificently, its hooves sending the gravel flying.

From below came two quick shots, the rounds whining off a cliff face beside him. He glanced back. It was Peterson on his mount. There was no sign of Earl. Longarm ducked lower in the saddle and urged the gray up the wash. It responded gallantly, but despite its great heart, it was beginning to falter. He could feel its flanks quivering under his thighs. Turning, he flung two shots at Peterson, hoping to slow him down some. The gray continued its charge up the watercourse for another fifty or so yards, then faltered, the gray's entire body shuddering. Longarm leaned over and patted the exhausted animal's neck to encourage it, then urged it on.

For another fifty yards it kept on, then stumbled, and with a shrill whinny of despair, collapsed on its side, its eyes wide and staring, streamers of lather billowing from its gaping mouth. Leaping clear, Longarm snaked Haskins's rifle out of its sling, rested it on the horse's steaming haunch, and waited behind it for Peterson to get closer.

Peterson saw what Longarm was doing and jumped from his mount. The horse wheeled gratefully and leaving Peterson behind, picked its way swiftly back down the wash. Longarm sighted on Peterson and squeezed off a shot. His round whined off a rock beside Peterson, who promptly dove behind a man-sized boulder. Resting his finger on the trigger, Longarm waited for Peterson's head to poke up. When it did, he sent a round that took a bite out of the boulder inches from Peterson's chin.

Peterson ducked back out of sight.

Longarm left the gray, scrambled up the wash a few hundred more feet, then found some cover and cranked the Winchester. But the rifle's magazine was empty. He flung the rifle aside, drew Haskins's revolver, and waited. In a moment Peterson came in sight. Longarm opened up on him. As Peterson dove for cover, Longarm turned and made for the rim.

He had not gone far before Peterson's rifle fire forced him to take cover in among some rocks. Peering down the wash, Longarm fired back at the oncoming Peterson, but Peterson was out of the sixgun's range. So Longarm held his fire and waited patiently for Peterson to get within range. But as soon as Peterson realized what Longarm was about, he held up and took cover, opening up on Longarm's position with his rifle. The lead flew about his head like angry hornets. Longarm flung himself to the ground, and as he waited for the fusillade to die, he took this opportunity to reload.

When Peterson ran out of ammunition and paused to reload, Longarm lifted his head and peered down the wash at Peterson.

"It's a standoff, Peterson!"

"Like hell it is!"

"Go on back down. If you do, I won't fire on you."

"Thanks for nothin'," Peterson snarled. "You can't reach me with that sixgun."

"Suit yourself. I ain't moving. You want to sit here all day?"

"Why not? I got plenty of time."

Longarm considered Peterson's response. The man sounded confident—too damn confident. Yet didn't he realize that when darkness came, it would be a simple matter for Longarm to slip on up to the canyon rim? And from that vantage point, the advantage would be all Longarm's. But that possibility did not seem to bother Peterson in the slightest.

Now, why was that?

Then Longarm thought of the deputy. He had forgotten all about Earl. He had seen him go down and had figured he was out of it. But that didn't have to be true. Hell. While Peterson was keeping Longarm pinned down on this slope, Earl could be making his way up to the rim by another route. And if he got there before Longarm did, they could take him.

Easy.

Longarm would have to get out of this pickle jar right now. He glanced up and studied the slope above him. On the other side of the wash, about twenty yards further up, there was a boulder large enough to shield him while he made a dash for the rim. The thing was to cross those twenty yards between where he was now and the boulder without getting his ass blown off.

He scrambled out from cover and dashed up the steep wash. Peterson's two rifle shots sent rounds burrowing into the gravel under his boots. He kept digging, and at one point went flat as the polished gravel slid out from under him. He reached out with his left hand, grabbed a projecting rock to halt his slide backward, then scrambled back up onto his feet. With gravel erupting inches from his flying feet, he finally gained the protection of the boulder. Glancing up, he saw the rim within a stone's throw. Keeping the boulder between him and Peterson, he continued on up the steep wash, grabbed hold of a gnarled bristlecone root, and pulled himself out of the wash and up onto the canyon's rim.

Jumping to his feet, he was was about to turn around to pick off Anderson when out from behind a juniper bush strode Earl. He was panting, his face bathed in sweat. It was clear the man had had to exert himself tremendously in order to reach the canyon rim before Longarm. Where his face had slammed into the ground earlier, it was a bloody mess.

But the revolver he was holding was steady enough.

"You don't look so good, Deputy," Longarm said.

Still panting slightly, Earl nodded grimly. "I near killed myself getting up here ahead of you, but it was worth it."

Longarm still had not lowered the sixgun in his hand.

"Drop the gun," Earl said.

Longarm did not do so.

"You heard me, damn it," Earl said angrily, thumbing back his Colt's hammer. "Drop it."

Longarm opened his fingers and let the gun slip to the ground at his feet.

"That's better. Now stay put."

Still covering him, Earl strode past him to peer down at Peterson, who was close enough for Longarm to hear him crunching up the gravel wash toward them. Earl grinned down at his partner.

"Hey! Come see what I got!"

As Earl called out, he took his eyes off Longarm. Longarm dropped to the ground, snatched up the sixgun, fired up at Earl and missed, rolled over once more as Earl fired wildly down at him, then sent a slug into Earl's chest. His sixgun still in his hand, Earl stared wide-eyed at Longarm, as if he couldn't believe what had just happened to him. He brought up his gun again, but before he could pull the trigger, Longarm sent a slug into Earl's breadbasket. Earl's gun thundered, sending a round into the sand at his feet. Then he toppled backward off the rim.

Longarm heard him strike the gravel, and hurried to the rim in time to see him tumbling down the chutelike wash. In an attempt to keep Earl from rolling on past him, Peterson grabbed the deputy's coat and hung on. But Earl's momentum was too great and Peterson was dragged down the wash after him.

Longarm watched until both men had tumbled out of sight, then turned away to go looking for Consuela and the ore wagon.

Chapter 6

"But I see you jump off the cliff!" Consuela said. "Then you come and untie me. How you do that?"

"The water broke my fall."

"You have the luck of the Devil, I tell you."

They were following the stream that had become a river, on their way to Needle Gap. Consuela, standing inside the ore wagon, was once more driving the team while Longarm rode alongside on a mount she told him had belonged to Amos. According to Peterson, the fat one had been shot by a Ute.

Longarm had retrieved his clothes, firearms, and hat, and was now completely dried off. He would have to peel out of his duds when he reached Needle Gap and plunge into a near-scalding hot bath. But for now he was reasonably content—if a little wary about Lars Peterson.

The son of a bitch was behind him somewhere, and the two would meet again.

"How about you?" Longarm asked Consuela. "You all right?"

"Them peegs use me, but I tell you for sure I give them no pleasure. First I am quiet, then I become like wildcat. They beat me, but they are such worms, they do not hurt me. Ortega, he is a real man. *He* know how to beat a woman."

"That so?"

"You not believe me? I still have his bruises."

"I didn't notice."

"I will show you." She looked at him, a light in her dark eyes. "Maybe later, when we get to thees town."

"I can't wait."

When they reached Needle Gap, Longarm found it just about as he had remembered it. The ramshackle, two-story hotel was easily as disreputable, the saloon as forlorn, and the feed and general store downright depressing. The stench of wet urine and horse manure from the livery stable was almost enough to raise his hair. As they passed the saloon, two unwholesome-looking gunslicks stepped out onto the saloon's low porch to watch the ore wagon rattle by. As they idly scratched their unshaven faces, their eyes lit hungrily on Consuela. Gleaming artillery hung low on their hips.

Consuela pulled the ore wagon to a halt outside the hotel. Longarm dropped his reins over the hitch rack in front of the hotel, then helped Consuela down. Inside, the hotel lobby was empty. Longarm slapped on the bell twice before a little old Ute Indian woman, her prunelike face inscrutable, came from behind a draped doorway.

"A room for the night," Longarm told her.

"Two dollar."

Longarm was going to complain about the cost, but said nothing and paid the woman. She lifted a key off a hook on the wall behind her.

"Room twelve," she said, handing it to him.

Longarm took the key and led the way upstairs to their room. It was a musty room, its two windows looking out onto the street. The brass bed was big enough, but it sagged in the center. He opened the window to air the room out, leaned out, saw nothing but dust and twilight, then stuck his head back in.

"I'm going back downstairs to see to the horses," he told her, "and get my gear out of the wagon. Then I need to find a place where I can soak this grime off."

"Ain't you had enough water, gringo?"

She was pouting, ready to show him her bruises—and whatever else was handy.

"I won't be long."

She shrugged. "It is no matter. I am in no hurry."

"When I get back we'll find a place to eat."

That brightened her a little, but not much.

He drew the wagon up on the other side of the street, near the livery stable, and unhitched the horses. Inside the barn he gave the old hostler more than he asked for to insure the man would give each of the horses a good rubdown, plenty of water, and sufficient oats. Then, lugging his gear with him, he found a barbershop across from the saloon, soaked for at least a half hour in a huge metal tub in back, and got a shave and a trim and put on a fresh shirt. He found that the only restaurant in town was in the back of the saloon, and went up to fetch Consuela and escort her into it. The restaurant's chairs and tables were set up in back. They ordered their supper, and found the food plentiful but greasy, the coffee strong enough to grow hair on a tit.

"Now, gringo," Consuela said, leaning back in her chair, her large luminous eyes regarding him somberly. "Are you ready now to go back to our room?"

"I think maybe I better finish this coffee first."

"You will not need it, I promise you."

"What's your hurry?"

"Do you not understand how I feel," she said, leaning forward, her voice sibilant with urgency, "after them cockroaches take me? I feel bad all over. My skin crawls when I think of them. They make a good thing bad. They make it filthy. With us it is not like that. I want you to wipe out the memory of their insolence. Make me feel clean again."

It was quite a speech, and Longarm was impressed. He had not realized how deeply Consuela had been affected by the rape she had suffered at the hands of Haskins and the others.

He reached over and took her hand, then smiled to reassure her. "Just let me finish this coffee first."

She took a deep breath, leaned back, and smiled back at him. "Of course. But hurry. This saloon, I do not like it so much."

Sudden, mean laughter erupted. Wincing impatiently, Longarm glanced in the direction from which it came. It was the same two characters he had seen on the saloon porch when he rode in. They had not taken their eyes off Consuela from the moment she entered with Longarm. The taller of the two was a white man, his companion a Mexican. They had been digging each other with their elbows while they kept up a steady drumbeat of sniggering comments on Consuela's obvious charms. Now, it seemed, they had taken to bursting into gleeful, coyotelike barks with every comment. Except for them and the barkeep, the saloon was empty.

"Them two jackals over there bothering you, are they?"

She shrugged, feigning an indifference she obviously did not feel.

"Well, they've been bothering me since we got here. Maybe I better go over there and have a chat with them. See if I can improve their manners some."

"No. Come upstairs with me."

"I still haven't finished this coffee, don't forget."

"Come on, gringo," she told him urgently. "We go now, huh?"

Giving in, Longarm finished his coffee and dropped enough coins on the table to take care of the meal. He stood up then and let Consuela lead him through the tables into the saloon portion of the establishment. Leaving Consuela, he drifted over a little in order to pass close by the table where the two gunslicks were sitting. As he reached them, their bearded, unwashed faces staring up at him, their mouths hanging open in derision, he kicked the table up into their faces. Both men flew backward, and the tall one went over in his chair, while his companion left his and landed heavily on the floor on his back.

As they landed, both men were drawing their sixguns. But Longarm had already drawn.

"Go ahead," he urged them coldly.

"Hey, what're you doin'?" the taller one whined as he stared up into the bore of Longarm's .44. "You got no cause to draw on us."

"No, I don't, and that's a fact."

"So why you do this?" demanded the Mexican. He was slowly, carefully easing his Colt back into its holster.

"You mean this ain't what you two assholes wanted me to do?"

"Hey, you think we crazy?"

"Now, that's funny. I thought sure you two jackals were deliberately trying to get me to draw—figurin' two against one would give you the odds jackals like you need."

On his feet now, the Mexican shook his head. "Hey, mister, you got us all wrong."

"No, I ain't. You got *me* all wrong."

"Hey, listen," said the taller one. He had a mean, foxlike face with eyes so pale they were like holes in his head. "What happened was, we mistook you for someone else."

The Mexican carefully righted the table and the two chairs. His companion pulled himself upright and slumped in his chair, the Mexican doing the same. Meanwhile, the barkeep, a sawed-off cue stick in his right fist, was hurrying over.

"What is this, mister?" he demanded of Longarm. "How come you drawin' on these two?"

"Nothing to worry about," Longarm told the man. "I was just sayin' hello to these two cockroaches." He stepped back and holstered his .44. "You got a license to run this place, have you?"

"A license? What in hell're you talkin' about?"

"I was just wondering. Seems a shame a classy establishment like you run here would serve such scum."

He walked over to the batwings, where Consuela was waiting, and escorted her from the saloon.

As Consuela flung off her clothes, Longarm crumpled up pieces of an old newspaper he had found lining a bureau drawer and dropped them on the floor in front of the doorway and then around both sides of the bed. After that he braced the back of a chair against the doorknob.

Then he undressed himself and joined Consuela on the bed.

Naked under him, she asked, "Why you do that to those men?"

"They bothered me."

"Now they will not leave us be."

"That's why I made these preparations." He slid his Colt under the pillow behind Consuela.

"You should ignore such dog turds."

"I thought you'd be pleased I put them in their place."

"Why should that be? I did not say anything about them."

"Yes, I wondered about that."

"I was thinking of you. I did not think you need any more trouble. Already you have suffered much. Did you not almos' drown? More trouble you do not need, I think."

"Thanks for looking out for me."

"But you are right," she admitted, smiling suddenly up at him. "I did not like those two. I hear some of what they say about me. It was not so pretty to hear this. But you surprise them good, take the smirk off their faces."

"Yes, I did at that."

"So, let us talk no more about them," she said, raising her arms to him. "Come into me, big man."

Longarm did as he was told, and for a long delicious while thought of nothing but pleasuring this woman and himself. When at last he finally cried uncle, she teased him some, but not all that much and with no malice at all—and looking into her eyes, he saw they too were heavy with sleep.

Embracing finally in one long sigh, they fell into a deep, trancelike slumber.

Early the next morning when Lars Peterson saw the ore wagon sitting outside the livery stable, he smiled in relief and turned his horse into the saloon's hitch rack. Inside the saloon, as he had expected, he found Grimes and Pedro. It was too early for breakfast, and they were sitting at a table covered with a checked tablecloth playing poker. They were waiting for the kitchen to open, he figured.

Grimes was the first to glance up from his poker hand as Lars approached. He spoke quickly to Pedro and both men, grinning, flung down their cards. Lars set a chair down beside them and chucked his hat back off his forehead.

"Thought maybe you'd got lost," Grimes said.

"Just rode in."

Grimes looked past him at the batwings. "You alone?"

"What's it look like?"

"Where's Haskins and the others?"

Lars told them.

"Shit," said Grimes, when Lars finished. "This here deputy sure is a troublemaker. He done cut your boys up and served them for dinner."

"He's lucky, that's all," said Lars. "And right now, I figure, his luck has ended."

Pedro shook his head. "I don't know about that. This gringo marshal is a real grizzly. He near ventilated me and Grimes last night."

"That so?"

"Yeah," Grimes said, his pale eyes smoldering. "We tangled."

"What happened?"

"We tried to rile him and Consuela while they was eatin' in here. It didn't get a rise out of him, we thought—then on the way out, he turned on us like a rattlesnake."

"I saw the wagon outside. Where is he now?"

"Upstairs with the wench." Grimes shook his head in admiration. "That sure is some woolly piece of tail."

Lars glanced over at the Mexican. "Did she let on she recognized you, Pedro?"

"Not that one."

"You think she'll warn him?"

"She didn't when she had the chance."

"What's she up to?"

"Don't you know?" asked Grimes. "She wants the gold too."

"Forget her," said Lars. "Right now, we got to take care of that big bastard upstairs. Thing is, we don't want no witnesses. He's a federal marshal, don't forget."

"I don't care if he's the King of England," said Pedro.

"What's the problem?" asked Grimes. "We just go on up there, kick the door in, and blast the son of a bitch."

"I don't like that," said Pedro. "With all that lead flyin' around, we might hit Consuela."

"So what," Grimes said. "All we need's one good look at her ass."

"No, my friend," said Pedro. "That might be all you need, but it ees not all I need. She will be my woman soon."

"Well, then," Lars demanded impatiently, "how're we going to take the bastard?"

"I think maybe I better talk to Consuela," Pedro said.

Grimes looked at him. "All right, you foolish son of a bitch. You do it. Go on up there and talk to her."

"Sure. I do that now. If she is awake, I will talk to her through the door."

"Don't talk crazy."

"Is not so crazy. Wait here, gringos."

When he came back to their table a few minutes later, Consuela was with him. At the sight of Peterson, she stiffened noticeably, her eyes raking him with such a cold contempt, he winced. He looked away from her and said nothing.

"Hurry up," she told them, sitting down at their table. "If Longarm wake up and find me gone, he will be suspicious."

Grimes said, "Just tell him you visited the crapper outside."

"What do you want?"

"The gold."

"You are fools. We do not have it."

"But you're going after it—and you have the only map." Grimes's pale eyes gleamed as he said this.

"So I have the map. What you want from me?"

"We're going to kill Longarm. We need your help."

"That is easy."

"You'll help us?"

"If you and Pedro will take me with you."

"Didn't take you long to turn on the bastard."

"I already tell you. I want the gold."

"Then you'll help us kill him?"

"I'll do it myself."

"How will you do it?"

She shrugged. "Is simple. I will kill the gringo while he sleep. With his own gun he keep under his pillow."

Peterson broke in, astonished. "You make it sound no more of a chore than combing your hair."

"And you'll do this for us?" asked Grimes.

"Fool!" she snapped. "I not do such a thing for you or this other gringo. I told you. I do this for the gold."

Pedro patted her arm to calm her, then glanced about at the others. "What do I tell you, gringos? This is some woman, eh? If she say she kill the lawman, she will do it."

Consuela got to her feet. "I go back now. But you must load the wagons with many pick and shovel before we leave."

"Anything else?" Peterson demanded sarcastically.

"Yes," she snapped. "Provisions. Plenty of provisions. We will have to eat, no?"

"She's right," Grimes said, turning to Peterson. "We do need provisions. You got enough to cover that?"

"I guess."

"Good," said Consuela.

She left the table and swept out of the saloon.

After she was gone, Grimes turned to Pedro. "You think she'll do it?"

Pedro leaned back, a smile on his face. "If any woman can do it, she can. I tell you, she is one wildcat."

"What about the gunshot?" asked Peterson.

"In this place," said Grimes, "all it'll stir up is the pigeons feeding on horseshit."

"When we get our hands on them gold bars, she's going to get her reward," Peterson said, grinning. "I'll see to it myself."

"Hey," Pedro reminded him. "You forget something. She is my woman now. You will have to stand in line!"

The three men roared with laughter.

Longarm woke to the feel of a rope tightening around his right wrist. His eyes flew open. But when he tried to sit up, he found his ankles and arms had been tied to the bed's four brass posts. He was spread-eagled on his back, as naked as a plucked turkey and just about as helpless. Bending over him was Consuela. He had been dreaming of her on top of him, whispering blandishments in his ear, and he had been struggling to wake up and take advantage of her.

"What the hell!" he cried.

She stuffed a piece of torn cloth into his mouth, then wrapped his bandanna over his mouth and behind his head to make it impossible for him to spit out the gag.

She straightened then to inspect her handiwork.

"I am sorry, Custees," she told him. "But I do this to save your life."

Longarm tried to pull himself free, but succeeded only in rocking the mattress. Consuela watched his efforts to free himself, obviously pleased at how well she had bound him. Then she rummaged through his frock coat pulled forth his pocket knife, and thrust it into her skirt's deep pocket. Watching her, Longarm realized he had never felt so damned helpless in his life.

Especially when she took his Colt from under his pillow.

Holding the weapon in both hands, her fingers around the trigger, she aimed playfully down at his crotch, closed her eyes, and then lifted the gun and blew a hole in the wall over his bed. The thunderous detonation in the small room was deafening; the recoil almost tore the gun from her grasp.

"Hey, I not expect such a recoil," she told him.

He frowned up at her, trying to get her to give him some kind of explanation. She understood his frown and leaned close, the smoking gun still in her hand.

"That shot won't bring no one. Thees town have no law. But now Lars Peterson and the others, they will think you dead—that I haf kill you."

Again he frowned.

"This morning Peterson join them two you mess with in the saloon. They want to come up here and kill you, but I say I do it. They are very stupid men, I think. But they dangerous all the same. Pedro is the Mexican. He is brother to Ortega. When we get the gold, Pedro say he will take me to San Francisco!"

She leaned quickly forward and kissed him on his forehead.

"See? Do not be angry. Thees way you no get hurt."

She dropped his gun onto the floor and hurried from the room.

Chapter 7

Later Longarm heard the door to his room open. He turned his head to see the old Indian woman, key in hand, entering. She stopped in mid-stride when she saw him, then pushed the door shut behind her and hurriedly crossed the room to his side, her walk a kind of eager shuffle. As she leaned over him and beheld his erect member, her prunelike face softened and her years seemed to melt away.

He had been doing his best not to foul himself, and as a result he had grown rigid—not with desire, but with a need so fierce it was all he could do to keep his bladder from bursting. But it was the old Indian's need that drove her now as she hitched up her skirt and hopped with amazing dexterity up onto the bed. Grinning with toothless abandon, she planted herself atop his erection, then wiggled down as far as she could get. Her weight was no more than that of a dried-out old bird, but the increased pressure on his bladder caused him considerable discomfort. He humped and twisted wildly in a desperate attempt to throw her off. But the old crone hung on gleefully, enjoying every damned minute of it, her flapping skirts and leather vest covering him with dust.

At last, his rage at being taken advantage of in this fashion invested him with a near-Herculean strength, and with one fierce yank he managed to bend slightly the top of the right rear bedpost. Since Consuela had had to loop the rope high on this post, it slipped over the top and his right hand was free. With one terrible wallop, he sent the old crone flying off him. She hit the floor and skidded to the open window, the back of her head rapping smartly against the windowsill. Looking like an oversized rag doll, she lay with her legs splayed out, her head sagged forward.

He ripped off the bandanna and spat out the gag. With his right hand, he lifted the rope that held his left wrist over the bedpost. Thrashing his legs wildly, he managed to loosen the ropes wound around his right foot. He pulled free, and a second later he was hopping on one foot and reaching under the bed for the chamber pot.

As he finished relieving himself, the Indian woman regained consciousness and uttered a faint mewling cry. Longarm untied his left foot and started toward her, his eyes cold with anger. As she saw him approaching, she shrieked like the fierce old bird she was and jumped up and tried to break past him. He grabbed her arm, but she broke away and ran to the open window, as if to fly out.

He caught her about the shoulder, then the neck—and for a moment he actually considered wringing it.

Sheriff Jed Newland had just made up his mind to ride back to Red Horse. He was saddle-sore and weary, and he was looking forward to his own bed—and his own town.

Close to noon the day before he had come upon the black, unholy cloud of buzzards ravaging the corpse of his deputy. There was another corpse as well, with its throat slit, that of the man named Haskins. Earlier on, he'd found another one, the short fat gent, shot dead and scalped, close by three other Mex corpses. If that scalped fat man wasn't enough warning, later yesterday, before descending to the trace leading into Needle Gap, he'd looked back and seen a line of three mounted Utes watching him from a ridge. They'd been within easy rifle range, and as he'd kept on into Needle Gap, the skin between his shoulder blades had been twitching.

He'd ridden in late that morning and had just finished a greasy breakfast that now sat heavily in his stomach, and was riding out, wondering if he hadn't been crazy chasing Earl this far. But, what the hell, he knew the son of a bitch was dead, and that gave him considerable satisfaction. Snugging his hat down more securely, he lifted his horse to a trot, and was passing the hotel when he heard a wild, terrified scream coming from just above him. Looking up, he saw Longarm holding an old Indian woman halfway out the open window, his big hands tightening on her scrawny throat. The U.S. deputy appeared ready to throttle the old crone.

"Hold it there, Longarm!" the startled sheriff cried.

"What're you doin' to that woman?"

Still holding her, Longarm looked past the Indian's struggling head at Newland. The sight of the sheriff seemed to shake Longarm out of whatever craziness had taken hold of him, and he immediately pulled back and flung the woman into the room behind him.

"Don't get riled, Sheriff," Longarm called down. "Just teaching her a lesson."

"What'd she do, for Christ's sake?"

"Never mind that. How long you been in town here?"

"Just got in."

"Where you headed?"

"Back to Red Horse."

"You mind holding up some? I think maybe you and me better talk."

Newland nodded. "All right. I'll ride on down to the saloon. Meet you inside."

"Much obliged."

It was a good half hour later before Longarm pushed through the saloon's batwings and entered the saloon. He caught sight of Newland waiting at a rear table and strode across the near-empty saloon toward him. Watching him approach, Newland was conscious once again of just how powerful an hombre this lawman was. He moved spooky quiet for a man his size, and seemed fashioned entirely of sinew and bone, carrying not an ounce of waste tallow. Judging from the flare of his well-oiled mustache, the deputy had spent some time in front of his mirror.

Reaching the table, Long stuck out his hand. As Newland shook it, he thought he noticed a fresh rope burn on his palm, but made no mention of it.

"Glad you showed up when you did," Long said.

He pulled over a chair and slumped down into it, waving over the barkeep who served as the establishment's cook. He ordered steak, fried potatoes, and eggs. The barkeep listened to all of it, then told Longarm all there was left was flapjacks and eggs. With a shrug Longarm ordered a stack of flapjacks and told the barkeep to scramble at least four eggs, ending with a demand to bring on the coffee at once.

As the bartender hurried into the kitchen, Longarm dropped his hat onto an empty chair and glanced at Newland, his open smile disarming. "After what I just been through, I need nourishment."

"No need to apologize, Longarm," Newland said. "I s'pose you got to stoke the furnace if you want steam in the boiler."

"Yeah, and right now I need plenty of steam." He fixed Newland with his gun-metal blue eyes. "I think I know what you came out here for, Sheriff. That renegade deputy of yours."

"The son of a bitch nearly killed me."

"How so?"

"I was set to take Haskins into custody when he came up from behind and unloaded on me with the barrel of his sixgun. Now I've told you my sad story. You want to tell me what happened to the son of a bitch?"

So Longarm told him. As he finished his account, his flapjacks and scrambled eggs arrived, along with a pot of coffee and two cups. Longarm paid the barkeep, poured Newland's coffee and his own, and then set to work on his breakfast with the urgency of a man who'd spent a winter living on a harness.

"That's quite a tale," said Newland. "From the sound of it, you're a very lucky man."

"That's what Consuela said."

"Which reminds me. Where the hell is she?"

"She lit out with Ortega's brother."

"Jesus. She got away from you, did she?"

"She did it to save my life, she said, but she left me in a very . . . vulnerable position."

"How's that?"

"Never mind. Anyway, she left with Ortega's brother, another gun-slick—and Lars Peterson. Ortega's brother and the other one were waiting here for Peterson, and I was too dumb to realize it. That gold is sure as hell drawing a crowd."

Longarm used his fork to slice down through his stack of flapjacks. Though he had just eaten, Newland was getting hungry all over again watching Longarm stow away his vittles.

"Longarm, maybe now you could explain to me what you were doing with that old squaw."

Longarm swallowed some flapjack, peered at Newland for a moment, then flushed the flapjack down the chute with a huge gulp of coffee.

"You want the truth?" he asked.

"Of course."

"She tried to rape me."

Newland waved his hand. "All right. All right. You don't have to tell me. So what was it you wanted to see me about?"

"Thought maybe we could throw in together."

"You want to spell that out?"

"Sure. I want you and me to go after the gold together."

"Why?"

"Because you know this country a damn sight better than I do. And right now I don't have a guide. I remember that map on Consuela's backside clear enough, but after Needle Rock, there really wasn't much to go on. Near as I can figure, there's two canyons west of here. One is due west and another one beyond it. This second one is the longest, and that's the one where the gold is supposed to be cached."

"That'd be Ute Canyon," Newland said.

"You know it?"

"I know it."

"So help me find it then. Throw in with me. We could cut cross-country and overtake them. What do you say?"

"You got quite a reputation, Longarm. You know that?"

Longarm shrugged.

"I never thought I'd hear the great Longarm askin' me for help."

"Any man don't ask for help when he needs it won't last long enough for it to do him any good."

"That's a fact."

"Well?"

"Sure. I'll ride along. What the hell."

"Good," Longarm said, finishing his last flapjack and reaching for the pot to pour himself and Newland another cup.

"One more thing," Newland said.

"What's that?"

"I found three dead Mexicans around a campfire and another one, just a kid, off in the brush by a cliff face.

And another one the buzzards brought me to on top of a butte."

"Them fool Mexicans tried to steal Consuela and the ore wagon."

Newland leaned back in his chair and shook his head incredulously. "Godamighty, Longarm. You realize what you done?"

"I had no choice, Newland."

"You don't have to apologize. Them five greasers've been picking off ore wagons for more than a year now. Earl and I never got nowhere trying to track 'em."

"Fine," Longarm said, leaning back and wiping his face with a napkin as he reached for his coffee. "I'm glad I helped get them out of your hair."

"You did that, all right. Now, once more. Will you level with me?"

"I already have."

"I mean about that business up in your room just now. Why in the hell were you attacking that squaw?"

Sipping his coffee, Longarm smiled at him and leaned back in his chair. "I already told you."

Dan Two Feather and the two members of his war party had watched the ore wagon leave Needle Gap, escorted by three riders and driven by the Mexican woman. One of the three riders was the only one remaining of the four who had killed their brother and spat on his forehead. But the gunfighter who had cut down the banditos was not with his woman.

Keeping to the rocks high above the trail, the Utes followed the ore wagon for a short while, then pulled their mounts to a halt and dismounted to discuss their next move. They were troubled. They had assumed the Mexican woman was the gunfighter's woman, but here she was riding out with these three men.

They sat on a flat rock, cross-legged in the warm sun, their faces held high so as to catch most of the steady, cooling breeze that came from off the snow-capped peaks surrounding them. Dan Two Feather was thinking of his own woman back at the agency. He could almost smell her on the wind.

In their own tongue they discussed the situation. Joe Big Hat spoke first. "The tall gunfighter is dead."

"Why do you say that?" asked Billy Indian.

"The woman has left him behind. And now she is allied with our enemy and his. I say the woman killed him."

"It is true," said Dan Two Feather. "These Mexican women are fierce. They kill like men. But I do not think she killed him."

"Why do you not think so? Did we not see her slit the young Mexican's throat?"

"She is very fierce," agreed Joe Big Hat.

"Still, I do not think she killed the gunfighter," said Dan Two Feather.

"Then why does she leave him and take the big wagon?" asked Joe Big Hat. He had taken off his Stetson and was fanning himself.

"Because she is a woman," Billy Indian said. "Do you need to know more?"

Dan Two Feather said, "It is gold."

"What gold?"

"Why do you think they go this far with the big wagon? It has high sides, like those that bring back the ore from the mines."

"Yes. That must be it," said Joe Big Hat. "They go after gold."

"So now we must go after the gold ourselves," said Billy Indian.

"What do we want with gold?" demanded Dan Two Feather.

"It is the white man's magic. I have seen how they bow before this yellow metal," said Billy Indian.

"It is the white eyes' sickness."

"If we take the gold, it will give us powerful medicine. I have heard of Indians living north of here in the green land high in the mountains, near the land of the red jackets. They build cabins like the white man, plant corn, and even keep horses they sell to the settlers who come through their land. With this money we could do the same."

"This is dream talk."

"It is better to have such dreams than to wake up each day with nothing before us but the coughing sickness."

"Tell us what you think, Two Feather," said Joe Big Hat.

Dan Two Feather thought over Billy Indian's words. His words had said what Dan Two Feather had been thinking, but only dimly. Going back to the agency was unthinkable. No more would he allow himself to become a blanket Indian. The gold might help them after all. Perhaps with it they could buy back their women from the agency. Dan Two Feather straightened his shoulders and cleared his throat. Billy Indian and Joe Big Hat waited.

"We will wait until these three and the Mexican woman reach the gold they seek," Dan Two Feather announced. "Then we will take the gold for ourselves."

Billy Indian and Joe Big Hat brightened. At last they had a purpose. No longer would they be aimless renegade Indians fleeing from a death-in-life-existence in a Utah agency.

The three Utes got to their feet and mounted up.

Chapter 8

Pedro had unrolled his blanket well above the campfire, and was leaning his head back against his saddle when he heard someone moving lightly across the slope toward him. He threw his blanket aside and stood up as Consuela materialized in the darkness before him. Her dark, luminous eyes peered at him intently, angrily.

"I do not theenk I like you anymore," she said.

Pedro scratched his head. "Why do you say that now?"

"You and them other two peegs. You treat me like whore."

"Hell, you didn't mind, Consuela. Besides, we was just looking that map over."

"No. You use that for excuse—you and them two cockroaches."

"Hell, what're you complaining about? You don't mind." He grinned. "Consuela, you are one woman who ees always in heat."

She slapped him so hard he felt his eyes water. Instinctively, his fist lashed out, catching her on the point of her chin. She staggered back, then regained her balance and was on him like a tigress, clawing and kicking, her fingernails reaching for his eyes. Laughing, he caught both her hands in his and squeezed—hard. Tears welling into her eyes, she sagged to the ground.

"I'll let your hands go," he told her. "If you promise not to come at me again."

Her head down, she nodded.

He let her go and leaned back against a boulder. "All right. I'll tell them two no more looks at your pretty ass. Besides, we don't need it anymore."

She got to her feet and brushed off her skirt. Looking at him intently, she said, "Why you not need the map anymore?"

"Ortega tell me he hide the gold inside an old mine shaft. But he did not tell me which canyon. Now I know which canyon. I see it on your ass."

"Have you tell the others this?"

"Hell, no. Why should I tell them?"

Consuela's eyes narrowed. "What are you going to do?"

"Don't you know?"

"Kill them?"

"When the time comes."

"This will be dangerous."

"You want to go to San Francisco?"

"Of course."

"Then let me handle it."

"If you keep them off my ass."

"Does that go for me?"

She shook her head and stepped into his arms. With an inward sigh he bore her down beneath him onto his blanket. It looked like he wasn't going to get as much sleep as he had counted on.

Consuela turned the horses into the shadow of the canyon's southern wall and pulled the wagon to a halt close in under it. They had just entered the canyon less than an hour before. It was wider by far than the one they had cut through two days before. This one had sheer walls towering much higher, and the floor of the canyon was wider with a broad, meandering stream cutting through it. There was brush and pines along the base and willows along the stream's banks. At the moment the sun was resting on the canyon wall just ahead of her. For most of the past three hours she had been shading her eyes with her left hand and holding the reins with her right, and had been relieved when Pedro rode past a moment before and indicated with a quick nod that he wanted her to stop here.

Ahead of her, she saw Peterson and Grimes circle and ride back to the wagon. She wrapped the wagon's ribbons around the brake handle and waited.

Peterson yanked his horse to a halt beside the wagon. "What're you stoppin' here for?"

"I am tired," she told him.

"Dammit! Keep going," he said. "We got some daylight left. An hour, at least."

Consuela ignored him and prepared to climb down out of the wagon. "All right, gringo. You drive the wagon. I have been standing all day while you ride on that horse."

"Maybe she's got a point," said Grimes, eyeing her hungrily. "We sure don't want to do nothin' to wear her out."

"Yes, I have a point," she retorted, climbing down from the wagon. "I have two of them—but you will not feel either one this night."

Grimes chuckled nervously and glanced over at Pedro, who had just ridden up. Pedro dismounted quickly and took Consuela's hand to help her down. It was a quiet but unmistakable indication of where he stood concerning Consuela and her charms.

"All right," Lars said, giving in. "We'll get an early start first thing in the morning." He glanced at Pedro. "Is this the right canyon, Pedro?"

"Might be."

"If it is," said Grimes, "we better take a good look at Consuela's backside tonight. Get ourselves a better look-see at that spot where Ortega hid the stuff."

"You see my ass enough," Consuela spat.

"Never mind," Pedro told Grimes. "I'll look it over for you."

"Yeah? Well, this time you better come up with something we can use."

"And if I don't?"

Grimes grinned. "Then we'll just have to skin the lady and take her ass with us."

"You just try, gringo!" Consuela snarled.

"All right!" said Peterson. "All right. Settle down, you two. Time now to get a campfire going. I'm ready to eat a horse. We don't want to rile our cook, do we?"

Consuela was about to say something more, but Pedro's fingers tightened about her arm, warning her.

She relaxed. No sense causing trouble now, she realized. Maybe tonight Pedro would kill these gringos and she would be rid of them for good. She would help him.

It took two hours before she was done feeding the three, after which she busied herself cleaning the pots and pans in the stream, then packing them up along with the provisions and storing them back into the wagon. The two gringos had eaten their fill and more than their fill, and had already found suitable spots for their blankets. Restless, nervous, she went back to the stream to wait for Pedro to join her. She found a grassy spot and sat down. The presence of the hobbled horses cropping the rich grasses near the stream comforted her somewhat. The only light now was the moon lifting above the western peaks.

She heard footsteps behind her. Pedro, she thought. But before she could turn, a rough hand closed about her mouth, while another caught her arm and twisted it cruelly up behind her back. She tried to twist away, to escape the awful pain, but this only increased the upward pressure on her arm. Realizing she was caught, she stopped struggling, her eyes closed, tears coursing down her cheeks from the pain.

Slowly, carefully, her attacker lessened the upward pressure on her arm as he turned her around, still keeping his hand clapped tightly over her mouth. It was Peterson. Grinning, he released his hand from her mouth and held a cautionary finger up to his mouth.

"You!" she hissed.

"Restless, are you?" he asked softly, grinning. "Coming out here all by yourself. In heat, maybe?"

She slapped him. He punched her in the gut. She doubled up in sudden, gut-wrenching pain. He caught her in his arms and again clamped his hand over her mouth.

"Let out one sound," he whispered, "a scream, a yell—anything, and I'll wring your lovely neck."

She nodded to indicate she would not call out. He removed his hand.

"What you want, gringo?" she hissed.

"Now ain't that the silliest damn question you ever asked?"

He grabbed her hand then and yanked her toward the canyon wall. A moment later, they came upon a narrow game trail. Without pause, Peterson pulled her up the trail after him. Not until the canyon floor was far below him did she manage to pull free.

"I will go no further with you," she told him heatedly.

"Why you so shy all of a sudden? You know you want it."

"You stink," she hissed. "You know that?"

He grinned. "Hey, none of us is perfect."

She looked into his face and realized that, at least for now, there was nothing she could do but go along.

Grabbing her wrist again, he said, "Come on. I found a nice spot up here. We ain't got far to go."

She let him pull her along, and it was not long before they came to a small flat, bordered by a stand of scrub pine. The moonlight slanting through the branches dappled the pine-carpeted floor. With someone she wanted—Longarm or Pedro—this would have been a nice spot. But with Peterson the prospect of what lay ahead filled her only with a deep revulsion.

Without a preamble of any kind, he threw her roughly down onto the pine needles, unbuckled his gunbelt and let it drop to the ground, kicked off his boots, and then peeled out of his pants.

Consuela watched him, saying nothing. In an apparent surrender to his demands, she pulled her dress up to make it easy for him. Naked from the waist down, he dropped beside her and thrust aside her thighs.

"Afterwards," he told her, chuckling, "I'll be wanting some information—more than I can find on your ass."

"Information? I don't have no information."

"So you say. But I got a hunch."

"You talk crazy."

"Yeah? Well, you and Pedro been pretty close lately. The way we figure it, you and Pedro know more'n you're tellin'."

"You are a fool to think that."

"Yeah? Well, we'll just see about that. Now, let's see what we got here."

She could see he was up now, and saw the eager gleam in his eyes. He slipped over her left thigh and was about to enter her, when she abruptly pushed him back with both hands and slammed shut her thighs, then jumped to her feet. With a bitter, angry curse, he scrambled to his feet and reached out to grab her. She lashed out with her foot, catching him in his hairy crotch, her toes digging hard into his balls. He uttered a low, agonized moan, and dropped to the ground, twisting and writhing as he clutched at his groin. Pleased, she watched him a moment, then picked up his gunbelt, his boots, and pants and hurled them down into the canyon. His boots landed near the stream, spooking the horses. Hobbled though they were, she heard them splashing farther down the stream.

She turned back to Peterson. He was on his feet now, still in pain. He had a long knife in his hand and his eyes were crazed with fury. For the first time in her life Consuela realized she might have gone too far.

"I'm going to finish with you right here," he told her. "Then I'll take you. Dead or alive, it don't matter to me."

She was shocked, aware that Peterson meant every word. "You kill me, you have no information," she reminded him.

"We still have Pedro," he muttered. "We'll cut off his ears, one at a time. He'll talk then."

"You are crazy. He know nothing."

"Bullshit!"

He started for her, his eyes wild with fury. It would do her no good to cry out now. It would only endanger Pedro as well. She took Longarm's knife from her skirt pocket and brandished it. It was short and would be little protection from Peterson's long, wicked knife. But she had no choice. She crouched, ready to sell her life dearly.

From the pines behind Peterson an old Indian stepped. He was dressed like a white man mostly, with a Stetson, cotton shirt and vest, and Levi's with a hole cut in them for his breechclout. In one stride he reached Peterson, dropped his arm around his neck, then shoved a knife into his back. Peterson did not cry out. His eyes widened in surprise, then lost all focus in death. The Indian let

Peterson topple to the ground, then bent over him and in one swift, expert motion, circled his scalp with the point of his knife and snapped off his scalp.

He straightened up then and looked at her. What passed for a smile eased the many lines on his old dark face.

"You fight well," he told her. "You have Indian blood?"

"Sure," she lied, nodding quickly. "Apache."

"Where is the gunfighter? You leave the town without him. Is he dead?"

"No," she said, aware he was referring to Longarm.

"He still lives?"

"Yes."

"He is a great warrior and you are his woman. Maybe you will find him again. I do not think you are safe with these men."

He turned and vanished into the trees. Consuela listened for the sound of his passage, but heard nothing. It had all happened so fast that for an instant she doubted it had happened at all. Then she looked down at the scalped Peterson and no longer had any doubts. But what should she do about his scalped corpse?

She decided the best thing would be to do nothing.

She picked her way back down the trail to the campsite and found Pedro asleep. She tapped him on his shoulder. He awoke, saw her, and with a sigh, opened his blanket for her. She settled down alongside him, but as he reached under her blouse and took her breast in his hand, she pushed his hand away.

"What's wrong?" he asked, sitting up.

She sat up also. "Peterson is dead."

"Dead?"

"An Indian killed him."

"Jesus. Where is he?"

"The Indian?"

"No, Peterson."

"Up there on the side of the canyon wall—without his scalp."

"You make no sense, woman."

Consuela told him how Peterson had dragged her up to a spot he had found, and all that happened once they got there.

When she had finished, he sighed and reached for his hat.

"Where you goin'?"

"To go up and get his body."

"No," she hissed. "Leave him. The gringo tried to rape me. Let the vultures feed on him. Besides, what can we do for him now? Let Grimes find him. We do not need to get involved."

Pedro put his hat back on the rock beside him. "Yeah, maybe that's what we'll do. Sometimes, you make good sense, Consuela."

She nodded quickly. "Now, all we have to worry about is Grimes."

Pedro folded the blanket over them both. "An Indian, you say?"

"Yes, but he is gone now."

She snuggled close to Pedro and closed her eyes. But for a long while she did not sleep; and when she dropped off at last, the last thing she remembered was the dark impassive face of the Indian as he turned and vanished into the pines.

• • •

The next morning she was up before either Pedro or Grimes, busy preparing their breakfast. After a while the clanging of the pots awakened them, that and the smell of fresh coffee. They shrugged off their blankets and went off down the stream to tend to their toilets.

When Grimes came back, he was holding Peterson's boots. He hurried over to Peterson's soogan and found it had not been slept under.

"Hey!" he cried to Consuela. "Where's Peterson?"

"I don't know."

Pedro approached Grimes. "Whatsa matter? Peterson run off, did he?"

Pushing Pedro aside, Grimes hurried over to Consuela. "What happened, dammit?"

"What you mean?"

"You think I don't know what he planned last night?"

"What did he plan?"

"To take you down a peg, that's what."

"You mean to rape me."

"You can't rape a whore."

She flung the pot of coffee at him. It struck him heavily in the chest, the hot coffee erupting from the top, splashing over his chin and neck. He cried out and staggered back, brushing the scalding coffee off him. Then he lunged at her, grabbed her right wrist, and yanked her closer.

"Bitch! What'd you do to Peterson?"

By this time Pedro had reached them. Gun drawn, he grabbed Grimes and flung him around.

"Hey, gringo. Leave Consuela alone."

"You drawin' on me, greaser?"

"Sure. Why not."

Consuela smiled meanly at Grimes. "You know so much about your frien', Peterson, you go find heem yourself."

"Yeah," said Pedro. "Go find him."

Grimes spun about, splashed across the shallow stream, and headed directly for the game trail. Pedro and Consuela watched, waited—and then a moment later exchanged smiles when Grimes called down to them from high on the canyon wall.

"Someone scalped Peterson!"

When Grimes returned, his face white, he stormed up to Consuela. "He had his pants off! You was up there with him! He told me he was going to take you up there."

Consuela shrugged. "I cannot help what he tell you."

Pedro said, "Maybe he was getting ready to call Consuela up there when he was scalped. Maybe he should've been more careful."

"I don't believe you two."

"So maybe I scalped him, that what you think?" Consuela suggested, winking at Pedro.

"That's right, Grimes," said Pedro. "Maybe she did that. Maybe you better watch out."

Pedro glanced at Consuela. She had no trouble reading Grimes's thoughts. He didn't know whether to believe Pedro or not. One thing only was certain. Peterson was dead and his scalp had been taken. Things were getting too complicated for him. Watching his frightened eyes and seeing how Grimes was beginning to sweat, Consuela found herself wondering if perhaps she would have been wiser to have remained with Longarm instead of throwing in with Pedro and this dog turd.

She thought then of Longarm and the Indian's words: *Maybe you will find him again. I do not think you are safe with these men.*

Chapter 9

Longarm pulled his mount to a halt. Beside him, Newland pulled up also and chucked his hat brim off his forehead. They could see clearly the ore wagon across the canyon floor below them. An abandoned mine shaft was visible about fifty feet off the canyon floor. A collapsed trestle, a few abandoned shacks, and a tin-roofed stamping mill were all that remained of the mine's outbuildings.

Longarm was pleased he had enlisted the sheriff's aid. Newland had led him on a torturous, but almost direct route through the badlands to this canyon—and the abandoned mine shaft, a perfect place for Ortega to have cached the gold bars.

Sitting their mounts, they watched Grimes and the Mexican enter the mine. Piles of slag littered the canyon floor below the mine, where the ore wagon now stood. Standing beside the ore wagon, Consuela was peering up at the mine entrance, waiting for the two to come out with the gold. She could relax now, Longarm thought. Her dusky ass was no longer so all-fired essential—at least not for finding gold.

"We got here just in time for the party," said Newland.

"That's what it looks like, all right."

"You want to go down and join it?"

Grinning, Longarm looked at Newland. "Why don't we hold up awhile?" He glanced up at the sky. "It'll be dark soon. I figure by the time they get the gold loaded into the ore wagon, they'll be ready to make camp. We can move in then. It won't hurt to let them bust their asses a little."

"Couldn't agree more," Newland said.

They edged their horses back off the rim, dismounted, and unsaddled the exhausted animals. After tethering them, Longarm and Newland returned to the canyon rim to watch the labors of Consuela and her two helpers. Ortega had apparently not hidden the gold too far into the mine shaft, and the Mexican was already lugging the first gold bars down the slope. That would be Pedro, Longarm realized, the one Consuela said was going to take her to San Francisco. Where Lars Peterson was, Longarm had no idea, but he was obviously nowhere around or he would have been pitching in with the rest. Longarm watched Consuela help Pedro load the bars into the ore wagon, then watched the Mexican return up the slope to the mine. A moment later Grimes came down with another load.

Longarm and Newland sat down to watch.

It was past dusk when Grimes and the Mex finished lugging the gold bars down the slope to the wagon. Soon after, as the two lawmen had expected, a campfire was lit. Longarm and Newland saddled their mounts and, following a game trail off the rim, descended into the canyon's darkness. When they reached the canyon floor, they pulled their horses to a halt and looked across the canyon at the campfire's winking light.

"You come around on the other side," Longarm told Newland. "I'll come in from this side. Cover me."

Newland nodded. "Just give me a chance to get in position."

Longarm nudged his horse slowly across the canyon floor as Newland trotted ahead of him into the inky blackness. Once he was close enough to see clearly Pedro and the other one squatting in front of the campfire, he decided Newland had had enough time to get in position and lifted his horse to a lope, the sound of his mount's hooves echoing clearly now against the canyon's walls. Pedro and the other one jumped up and drew their guns, peering in his direction. Longarm could not see Consuela. Just outside the campfire's ring of light, Longarm halted and drew his .44.

"I can see you a whole lot better'n you can see me, gents," Longarm called to them. "Throw down your weapons."

"Who the hell are you?"

"U.S. Deputy Marshal Long."

"You're s'posed to be dead," cried Pedro.

"Don't you believe it," said Longarm, chuckling.

Both men swiveled their heads to look at the ore wagon.

"You bitch, Consuela!" cried the one standing beside Pedro. "You didn't kill him like you promised."

From the wagon came Consuela's taunt: "You fool, Grimes! You think I would murder such a man in cold blood!"

"No more palaver," said Longarm. "Unbuckle your gunbelts and drop them."

The two men peered in helpless frustration into the blackness beyond their campfire, then did as Longarm told them.

"Now, step away from them. Move!"

Pedro and Grimes took a few strides away from the guns and halted. A moment later, as Longarm urged his horse into the ring of light, Sheriff Newland entered also, coming from the opposite direction.

Only the gun in his hand was aimed not at Grimes and the Mexican—but at Longarm.

"Don't do nothin' foolish now, Longarm," Grimes said.

"What the hell!"

Newland shrugged unhappily, as if none of this were his idea. "I'm sorry to have to do this, Longarm," he drawled. "Now, please, just do as I say and drop that .44 to the ground."

Newland kept on riding toward him as he spoke. Longarm let the .44 fall to the ground.

"Now get off that horse and step away from it."

Longarm dismounted and walked away from the horse. Newland dismounted then and, keeping his gun leveled on Longarm, glanced at Pedro and Grimes.

"Don't you two get brave all of a sudden," he told them. "Get over here beside Longarm."

"What in hell're you up to, Sheriff?" Grimes asked.

"You mean you don't know? We just saw you two loading up this wagon with gold bullion."

As Grimes and Pedro moved over to stand beside Longarm, Newland sent a casual shot at the side of the ore wagon. As the slug slammed into the wooden side, Consuela cried out.

"Madman! What you do?" she cried to Newland, sticking her head up over the wagon's side.

"Never mind that," Newland told her. "Get over here."

She climbed to the ground and walked over, eyes smoldering.

"Get some rope," he told her, "and tie these three up."

As Consuela went to fetch the rope, Newland picked up the discarded sixguns, emptied them, then flung them into the wagon. Then he strode back to watch closely as Consuela bound the men's hands behind them. As Consuela tied Longarm's hands, she leaned close and whispered that she would not tie his wrists too tightly.

"What are you tellin' him, woman!" Newland cried, moving quickly toward her.

"I tell him I am his woman. What is it to you?"

Newland looked ready to take a swipe at her, then stepped back as Consuela continued to tie them.

"You gone loco, Newland?" Longarm asked him.

"No. For the first time in my life, I'm thinking clearly."

"You'll never get away with this."

"And I'll never get rich wearing a tin star either."

"Think a minute, Newland," Longarm said. "That gold belongs to Wells Fargo. What makes you think you can

117

use those solid gold bars for currency."

Newland smiled confidently. "I have an entirely different prospect, Longarm, somethin' I been ponderin' since you brought me into this. I'll be taking this bullion some distance from here to a gent I know who can melt the gold into negotiable coin."

"You sure changed fast, Newland," Longarm commented.

"Yeah. I noticed that myself. Don't take long in this country."

"Hey," Grimes broke in, "why be in such a hurry, Newland? Let's talk this over. We can work together."

"I don't deal with scum like you."

Pedro chuckled. "Well, gringo, you better get used to doin' it. You are one of us scum now."

"No more talk," Newland told them, stepping back to let Consuela work.

Once they were trussed to Newland's satisfaction, Newland told Consuela to hitch up the wagon's horses.

"Now listen," he told them as Consuela hurried off, "and listen good. I don't want no blood on my hands—not if I can help it. So I'm goin' to give you three some advice. Start back to Needle Gap on foot. You might get there and you might not. One thing for sure, though—if I see any of you following me and the wagon, I'll cut you down. And don't think I won't do it. Now, move out—all of you."

Longarm started walking, the others keeping behind him. In a moment they had passed beyond the campfire's light into the darkness beyond. They kept walking. Soon enough, they heard the jingle of harness accompanied by the deep rumble of the ore wagon as it began to move. Longarm turned to watch it go. Newland was barely visible riding alongside, Longarm's and his two companion's horses trotting just ahead of the wagon. Abruptly, Newland sent two shots over their backs and the horses immediately plunged on ahead of the wagon into the night, the pound of their hooves soon fading. Not long after, the rumble and groan of the ore wagon faded into the night as well.

Pedro and Grimes then turned to regard Longarm.

"Our fingers are free," Grimes snarled. "Just our wrists are tied. Pedro and me are going to untie ourselves. Then watch out, lawman."

Pedro backed up to Grimes and Grimes began the difficult but not impossible task of untying Pedro's bonds. Meanwhile, Longarm did his best to untie himself. As she had promised, Consuela had not tied the ropes too tightly; even so, it was not an easy task to loosen them entirely, and before his hands were free, Grimes and Pedro were striding toward him.

"You are one lucky man we ain't armed," the Mexican said.

"Or we'd just shoot you down like a dog," Grimes pointed out. "One thing I can't stand is a lawman."

"You going after Newland?" Longarm asked.

"That's right," said Grimes.

"On foot?"

"Sure," said the Mexican. "Them horses, they get tired out soon enough. We'll find them, mount up, and catch up to the bastard. We never did get around to unsaddling them. We was plumb wore out."

"It'll be a long trek before you catch up to them mounts."

"Well, it ain't your worry, lawman."

"Let me go along with you. Help me collar Newland and I'll see what I can do about the charges against you."

"What charges, gringo?" demanded Pedro.

"You ain't got no charges to drop," said Grimes.

"I could think of some."

"Yeah, I'll bet you could."

Grimes stepped close to Longarm and punched him in the face. Longarm staggered back, but remained on his feet. Grinning happily with the sheer delight he was feeling, Grimes followed up the first punch with another one to Longarm's midsection. Retching, Longarm sagged forward onto his knees. Measuring carefully, Grimes brought up his knee and caught Longarm under his right eye. Lights exploded in his head, and the next thing he knew he was lying on his back, staring shakily up at Grimes, who had danced eagerly to Longarm's right side and was drawing his foot back. Before Longarm could turn his head away, the point of Grimes's riding boot struck him in the side of his head, just behind his ear.

The night spun away in sickening circles. Grimes leaned close. Unable to move a muscle, Longarm tried to gather sputum in his mouth to send it at Grimes, but the blow had so completely paralyzed him he was unable to move a muscle. Grimes studied him for a moment, looking for any movement or sign of life, then kicked him viciously in the chest for good measure, then stepped back.

"Hey, you finish the bastard, all right," said Pedro. "But let me show you something."

Bending over him, Pedro flipped aside his frock coat and reached into the watch pocket in Longarm's vest.

He drew out Longarm's Ingersol railroad watch, and with it, the derringer fastened to the gold chain that was resting in the watch fob pocket. Unclipping the derringer from the chain, Pedro flung the pocket watch into the darkness and pocketed the belly gun. Then he leaned close, grinning at Longarm's frozen face.

"I know all about this here belly gun," he said, chuckling. "Ortega, my brother, he tell me."

He aimed the gun down at Longarm.

"What you doin' there?" Grimes demanded. "That belly gun only holds two rounds. We'll need both when we catch up to that sheriff."

"Don't you want to finish off this lawman?"

"I already done that. Look at him."

Bending close, Grimes slapped Longarm hard on both cheeks. When there was no response at all from the blows, Grimes straightened up, well satisfied with his handiwork.

Pedro leaned close and rested the derringer's double barrel on Longarm's cheek, then waited for Longarm to respond. When Longarm didn't, he spat in his face, pocketed the derringer, and walked off with Grimes, the sound of their footsteps soon fading into the night.

Longarm tried to move, but all the lines were down. He waited. After what seemed like a very long time, he felt a spark of life returning to his body. Before long he was able to close his eyes, then flex his fingers. A moment later he felt the cold spittle Pedro had planted on his cheekbone and knew he was going to be all right—but only because in the darkness Grimes's boot had missed Longarm's temple. If it had struck the area in front of his ear instead of behind it, the blow would have crumpled Longarm's skull like an eggshell.

He began to work on the ropes binding his wrists. He had already loosened them some; nevertheless, the exertion was almost too much for him. He kept losing consciousness. He persisted, however, and close to daybreak his hands were free. He sat up, got to his feet, and staggered over into the shade at the base of the canyon wall. There, in among a clump of pine, he found a grassy spot close against the cliff side, and dropping to it, passed out.

The sun was high when he awoke. Lifting his head, he shook it gently and was surprised that it did not fall off. From deep inside his skull came a dull, persistent throb, but it was not something he couldn't live with. He was alive, and that was all that mattered. He pushed himself upright, squinted out at the sun-blasted canyon floor, then got to his feet and left the pine to retrieve his hat, which was in plain sight near the edge of the stream.

He had to set it down gingerly onto his sore head, but with the task accomplished, he set about looking for his watch and chain. When he found them at last, he picked up the watch up and held it to his ear. It was still ticking. He then consulted it. Ten o'clock. Not yet noon. Good. He slipped the watch into his vest pocket, after unclipping the chain and dropping it into his frock coat's side pocket. Then he walked over to the burnt-out campfire and searched the ground for the shells Newland had emptied onto the ground. When Longarm found his .44-40 shells, he pocketed them and set out after Grimes and Pedro.

He kept on at an unhurried pace, following the canyon wall closely to keep out of the direct sunlight and making frequent visits to the stream to fill his canteen and dip his bandanna into the water. Wrapped around his head, and kept in place by his hat, the sodden bandanna helped greatly to soothe his skull's pounding.

Despite the discomfort, Longarm was not discouraged. Pedro and Grimes would not have walked through the night, and might well have slept over some before getting up this morning, which meant they might not be all that much ahead of him. Though he might not overtake them this day, if he kept going into the night, he was confident he would come upon their camp.

Longarm found Grimes and the Mexican camped close under the canyon wall. There were no horses hobbled near the stream, and that was a disappointment. On the other hand, had these two found the horses, they would have been long gone.

It was close to midnight. Their campfire was little more than glowing coals, but it gave off enough light for Longarm to be able to make out their sleeping forms. They were on the other side of the fire, sleeping with no cover and with no pillows. Longarm had already picked up a piece of dry wood to use as a club and carried it in his left hand as he picked his way carefully past the jagged boulders littering the ground beneath the canyon's rim. When he judged he was close enough to make an accurate toss, he threw three of his .44-40 shells into the campfire. Then he ducked back into the darkness.

He did not have long to wait. One of the shells detonated, then the other two, these in rapid succession. The sleeping men jumped up in a panic and without bothering to discuss the matter, Pedro ran for cover back toward the canyon wall, while Grimes ran straight toward Longarm. As he rushed past Longarm, Longarm brought his club down, aiming for Grimes's head. But in the darkness, his blow went awry, glancing off Grimes's shoulder instead. Grimes knocked Longarm to one side and kept on, then whirled and dug into his side pocket and came up with Longarm's derringer. Before he could raise it to fire, however, Longarm stepped in close and brought the club down across Grimes's right forearm.

The man cried out and Longarm realized he had broken the arm. But before he could close in, Grimes switched the belly gun to his left hand. Longarm grabbed the gun and twisted violently in an effort to wrest it away. For a moment the two men struggled wordlessly until Longarm crunched against Grimes's broken forearm. Grimes cried out and staggered back. Longarm lunged after him, slammed him back against a boulder, then yanked violently on the gun.

This time the derringer detonated, the explosion muffled by the two bodies. Grimes's face appeared to dissolve as the bullet entered just under his chin, coursed up through his nostrils, and lodged in his brain. As he stepped back to let Grimes sag to the ground, Longarm snatched the derringer from his lifeless hand.

Someone—Pedro, no doubt—was pounding through the night toward them. Longarm went down on one knee, turned toward the sound of pounding feet, swung up the derringer, and waited.

Out of the darkness plunged Pedro.

"Hey, Grimes. What is this?" he cried. "You take my gun!"

Longarm fired his remaining round. Pedro stumbled and went down like a horse stepping into a gopher hole. Longarm sprang forward to examine him. But before he reached him, Pedro jumped up and bowled past him, disappearing in among the rocks, apparently unaware that Longarm's derringer was empty. Longarm reached into his side coat pocket for more rounds, reloaded the derringer, then took after Pedro. But in the darkness he succeeded only in banging his shins on boulders and crashing blindly into saplings.

When he had sense enough to hold up and listen, he thought he heard movement in the rocks off to his left. But the sound faded so rapidly it was of no use to him. He gave up and returned to the canyon floor. As he neared the spot where he had downed Grimes, in the faint moonlight he noticed dark patches of blood on rocks and on a few sandy stretches left by the wounded Pedro. Kneeling to examine them, Longarm concluded that Pedro could not go far, not if he was losing this much blood. He would go after him at daybreak.

He trailed Pedro's spoor for almost a mile the next day before it ran out. Weary, his head pounding, Longarm halted and looked around him at the dismal, rock-strewn landscape. A few towering chimney rocks and buttes were the only formations that broke the monotony. He realized that Pedro could be anywhere in these bleak badlands, safely holed up while he licked his wound.

If he was still alive.

Longarm returned to the canyon and set out once more in search of a mount.

Chapter 10

It was noon the next day when Longarm came upon his chestnut. He was pleased until he found that the horse had thrown a shoe and severely bruised its frog. He took his saddle off the chestnut, then his saddlebags and saddle roll, and withdrew his Winchester, which still rested in its sling. Resting the saddle on his shoulder, he shifted it a couple of times to get it more comfortable, then trudged on. He was sure the chestnut's foot would heal in a matter of weeks. Thing was, if it fell in with a band of mustangs, it would more than likely take over the band before long, and never again would a human get close to the chestnut—or any member of its band.

Not until dusk, on a brush-pocked flat just beyond the canyon, did he come upon another of the stampeded horses, a powerful roan, cropping the grass close by the stream. As Longarm approached, the spooked horse swung its head up, its ears flat, its nostrils flaring, a crazy light in its eye. It looked to Longarm as if the roan was pretty close to going wild. But it was still saddled, its reins trailing, and Longarm was able to get close enough to grab them. The horse bucked a little, but calmed quickly enough and let Longarm lead it into the cool shadows close under the canyon wall, where he took off its saddle, groomed the horse for a while to gentle it, then slapped on his own saddle. Judging from the Spanish bit, the roan had belonged to Pedro.

Longarm swung into the saddle, and keeping close to the stream, rode on through the night. By daybreak, he was exhausted, looking for a campsite, when he saw a man coming toward him. He appeared to be staggering. He was not wearing a hat, but was too far away for Longarm to tell much about him.

Abruptly the man stumbled and collapsed facedown.

Longarm urged his horse on, and when he came up to him, he dismounted and bent over the prostrate figure. A familiar knife handle protruded from his back. He withdrew the knife and turned the man over, and was not surprised to find himself looking down at Sheriff Newland.

Newland's eyelids flickered, then opened. When the sheriff saw Longarm, he managed a wry smile.

"You're a brave man," he rasped. "I warned you what I'd do if I ever saw you again."

"Yeah. I remember. You're going to cut me down. Maybe you should've left Consuela behind with us."

"Jesus. That's sure some bitch."

"What'd you do—turn your back on her?"

"Hell, no. My back wasn't to her. We were humping like two crazed mink when she buried that knife in my back."

"She's a wild one, all right."

He tried to move a little to get comfortable. A thin trickle of blood was coming from one corner of his mouth. "I don't feel so good."

"How far ahead of me is she?"

"Don't know. I just came to a little while ago. Can't tell you much . . . I'm thirsty, Longarm. Dry as a bone."

Longarm pulled the man into the shade of some scrub juniper, unscrewed the cap on his canteen, placed its neck into Newland's mouth, and tipped it up. Newland gulped greedily at the water. After a moment, however, he began coughing and Longarm had to pull the canteen away. It was a rough, ragged cough that didn't sound so good. Newland nodded his thanks to Longarm and eased himself back onto the ground.

"Guess I'm gettin' what I deserve," he muttered. "Right?"

"You didn't hear me say that."

"Where are the others?"

"The Mex and Grimes?"

"Yeah."

"Grimes is dead. I'm not too sure of Pedro."

"You did it?"

"They didn't give me much choice."

"Jesus. This here gold . . . it's takin' a toll, ain't it."

"It is that."

"Anyway . . . I'm glad I didn't kill you—or the others."

"Maybe you should've."

"Aw, shit, Long. You know I couldn't've done that."

"Looks to me, Newland, like you don't have the proper attitude for an outlaw."

He smiled wanly. "Maybe not . . . but it's too late for that now."

"Don't give up, Newland," Longarm urged gently. "That was just my pocket knife she used."

"Didn't feel like a pocket knife," he said, "more like a branding iron ten feet long. Don't worry . . . won't hold you up much longer."

He closed his eyes wearily. Watching him, Longarm said nothing. He didn't feel up to it. After a moment Newland stirred and glanced up at Longarm.

"Hey, Longarm," Newland gasped. "I got a question."

"Sure. What is it?"

"That old Indian woman. What were you doin' with her?"

"I told you. She tried to rape me."

He grinned. "You . . . bastard."

"You don't believe me?"

He shook his head.

"Well, give me time. Maybe I'll come up with something you'll believe later. Just hang in there."

Newland closed his eyes and began to move restlessly. Longarm left him and walked out to the stream to refill his canteen. He hoped it might help some if he washed out Newland's wound and put a cooling compress on it. When he returned, Newland was lying on his side. The blood flowing out of his torn lung had turned his lips black. Longarm placed the back of his hand against Newland's cheek. It was cold. The fire was out.

He never would get to explain to Newland what had happened up in that hotel room.

• • •

Not long after burying Newland, Longarm was pulling himself across the top of a rock, peering down at the ore wagon. Consuela was close by it, busy building a fire. When he first caught sight of her, she had been driving the ore wagon in his direction, evidently on her way back to Needle Gap.

He had immediately tethered his horse out of sight and climbed into the rocks to wait for the wagon to pass below him. Instead of moving on by, however, Consuela had pulled the wagon in close to the rocks below Longarm and set about making camp.

Now he watched as she prepared her supper, marveling at the fluid economy of her movements. Even at this distance she was a very beautiful—if deadly—woman. After a moment, the coffeepot began to sing, and he could smell its strong aroma. He had not eaten in so long, his stomach was queasy and the smell of the beans, jerky, and hot peppers sizzling in her fry pan caused his jaw to ache. He decided he was ready to show himself.

He called down to her, then stood up on the rock and raised his rifle over his head to catch her eye. She turned and glanced up at him, shading her eyes from the lowering sun.

"Custees?" she cried.

She was obviously delighted. He could see the gleam of her smile even from this distance.

"Save me some coffee!" he called.

He clambered down the steep trail to his tethered mount. A moment later, riding up to the wagon, he found Consuela waiting for him with a steaming cup of coffee in her hand.

He dismounted and took the cup from her. He had to sip it at first. It was just what he needed. He handed back the empty cup.

"Thanks, Consuela."

She flung her sable hair back off her shoulders and put her hands on her hips. Shaking her head in wonder, she said, "You remember what I tell you, Custees? You are one very lucky man."

"I can't deny it," Longarm told her. He looked past her at the campfire. "I am also a very hungry man."

"Sit down. I feed you. Then we make love, hey?"

"Sure."

When they finished their supper, Longarm made an excuse to check the gold. He climbed up into the wagon and found his .44-40, along with the sixguns belonging to Grimes and the Mexican. He loaded his own double-action with the two cartridges left from those he had picked up off the canyon floor. He dropped the Colt into his cross-draw rig, then swung down out of the wagon.

Consuela was out by the stream, scrubbing the fry pan and tin plates with wet sand. He strolled out to her.

"I buried Sheriff Newland," he told her.

She put down the pan she was cleaning and glanced over her shoulder at him. "Why do you bother? Let the buzzards have him."

"Didn't want to do that."

"He was a peeg." She spat to emphasize her contempt.

"I already guessed you didn't like him."

"Like heem? He stink like an animal. He use his gun to make me satisfy heem. He give me no choice. But I do not lay with any man 'less I want to—or have no choice." She smiled suddenly. "So your knife, it give me a choice."

Longarm could find little to say in response and started back to the fire. Consuela stood up and called after him.

"I keel your frien', so now you hate Consuela!"

He stopped and turned around to look at her. "Now, how could I hate a woman who can cook like you?"

He was waiting for her smile. But it did not come. Without a word—or smile—she crouched back down beside the stream to finish cleaning the fry pan.

He walked over to the roan for his bedroll. Soon after he climbed under his soogan, Consuela materialized out of the night. She had on her skirt and blouse, but no sandals—and as usual there was nothing, he realized, under her blouse or skirt—except her warm, passionate body. But he did not fling aside the soogan to make room for her.

"You do not want me?" she asked.

"I am pretty damm tired, Consuela," he admitted. "I rode through the night, and before I found that roan, I walked near five miles carrying my gear—that includes my rifle and saddle."

"So you are too tired for Consuela."

"I didn't say that."

"You hate me because I kill your frien'."

"Newland was no friend of mine. But he was a lawman."

"Is that it? Because he pin a tin star to his vest, you must grieve for him? I think you are crazy, Custees. He was no good. He rob us of the gold, like any outlaw."

"Yeah, well, I *am* tired, Consuela."

She studied him through shrewd, narrowed eyes. "Maybe you are afraid of Consuela."

"A man who ain't afraid of a woman is a damn fool."

She softened then. "Maybe you right." Then she smiled. "But I do not have your knife now."

"I know. I took it out of Newland's back."

"Why don't you stand up and search me. Maybe I have other knife."

Longarm almost laughed aloud. "Never mind," he said.

"Go ahead. Search me. I will let you."

Wearily, he stood up and placed both hands on Consuela's hips, then moved them up to her full breasts, her sweaty cleft. Moving closer, he felt the back of her dress, then her blouse. Nothing. By that time he was no longer searching for a weapon—and as she thrust herself closer to him, he became intensely aware of her sultry, eager readiness for him.

She laughed softly and kissed him on his lips. Holding her in his arms, he lowered her to the blanket. She kicked off her skirt and tossed her blouse away. He settled into her and rested his head in her cleft, the sweaty heat of her body arousing him to a pitch that banished his fatigue.

"Ah," Consuela sighed, "there is so much of you, Custees!"

She widened her legs and helped him ease deeper into her tight, moist warmth. Longarm probed deep and then deeper as she shoved her pelvis up eagerly under him. When he struck bottom, she moaned and tightened her inner muscles, and for a delicious while they rocked together in a mounting spasm that swiftly lifted them over the edge. Crying out as Longarm pulsed inside her, she wrapped her arms tightly about him, hugging him close, her head flung back as she shuddered repeatedly under him. Only slowly did she relax. Watching her, he saw the flush on her dusky cheeks, the tiny beads of perspiration pebbling her face and soaring breasts.

She smiled at him.

"That was so good, Custees," she told him, her fingers stroking his hair; her lips brushed his forehead. "You are such a long man."

"And lucky too, don't forget."

For a long delicious interval they lay in each other's arms, while Longarm did his best to fight off the waves of fatigue that threatened to pull him into a deep, dreamless sleep.

"Custees?"

He opened his eyes. "What?"

"The gold, do we have to give it all back to Wells Fargo?"

"That's the deal. Besides, isn't that why you were taking it back?"

"Of course. I just ask you is all."

Longarm said nothing more and closed his eyes. For a while they remained clasped in each other's arms, Longarm's head resting in the bountiful fold of her breasts. After a while, close to sleep, he rolled off her onto his back.

With a chuckle, Consuela swung herself astride him. He looked up at her. She smiled down at him, triumph gleaming in her dark, liquid eyes.

"You not afraid of Consuela now?"

"As long as you're not armed."

Abruptly, she reached past his head and removed his Colt from the holster resting under his saddle. Holding the muzzle inches from his right eye, her finger coiled around the trigger, she shut one eye and seemed about to squeeze off a shot.

He had slipped only two rounds into the Colt, which made it better than a fifty-fifty chance the hammer would come down on an empty chamber, but he sure as hell wasn't eager to make that kind of a gamble. Besides, the gun was a double-action. All she had to do was keep the pressure on the trigger until the hammer found a loaded chamber. He thought of throwing her off him, but that would only increase the likelihood that the Colt would detonate.

"You afraid of Consuela now?" she asked.

"You're goddam right I am."

"You think I want to take the gold?"

"That's what I think."

"You are silly," she told him, bending suddenly forward and slipping the Colt back into Longarm's holster. "I will not take the gold. Besides, I would not shoot my beeg lover!"

Longarm sat up, inwardly furious. Consuela flung her arms about him. He kept his rage under control and did not push her away.

She whispered into his ear. "It is not fair men are the only one who carry gun. Don't you think?"

"I never thought of it."

"So just now I show you how it feel to be woman with no weapon to defend her."

"Thanks for showing me."

"I could have keel you."

"I know that."

"But I did not."

"I'm real grateful."

"So now you trust Consuela, eh?"

"Sure."

Her arms released him and she sat back so her eyes could meet his. "Ah, I can tell. You are unhappy with Consuela."

"You took advantage of me, Consuela. You made me sweat, and that's a fact. It was not a nice thing to do."

"It is true," she sighed. "Consuela is sometime a very bad girl."

"No. You got that wrong. Consuela is always a bad girl."

She frowned. "I not think I like that."

"I don't care what you like."

He drew her wearily down onto the blanket beside him. At first she held back, but only for a moment; she snuggled close against him.

"Now, let's get some sleep," he told her. "We got a long way to go yet."

He drew the soogan over them both. In a moment she was sound asleep. It took a while for Longarm to drop off, however, and when he did his right fist was closed about his Colt's grips.

Chapter 11

Two days later, skirting a canyon wall, Longarm and Consuela found their way blocked by three mounted Indians. Two of them had eagle feathers in their Stetsons, and leather vests decorated with conchos and copper bullet casings. They all wore Levi's, sleeveless cotton shirts, and gunbelts and holsters. A rifle rested across each pommel. The oldest one, most likely their leader, was trailing two saddled horses. Longarm recognized Newland's mount immediately. The other mount had belonged to Grimes.

Consuela yanked on the ribbons and stepped hard on the brake. The ore wagon skidded to a halt. Longarm had been riding alongside the wagon and promptly reined in his roan. The oldest Indian, the only one without a feather in his hat, nudged his horse to a walk and moved closer. His two companions remained back, their coal black eyes alert, their faces impassive.

Rearranging the lines on his face into what could have passed for a smile, the Indian pulled his horse to a halt alongside Longarm's horse and held up his right hand in greeting.

"The gunfighter has powerful medicine."

"Reckon that's so, Chief."

"You kill those who kill and insult our brother."

Longarm nodded, not entirely sure he knew what the Indian was talking about. But what was clear was that these three Utes must have been following Longarm—and the others as well—for some distance.

"How are you called, Chief?"

"I am Dan Two Feather. My brothers are Billy Indian and Joe Big Hat."

Glancing past Dan Two Feather, Longarm had little difficulty distinguishing between Big Hat and the other one. "What is it you want, Dan?"

"We come for the gold."

"You what?"

"You hear me."

"All right. I heard you. But what the hell do you want this gold for?"

"Why you surprise? Gold is strong medicine. It will help us buy land and live like white man. We will build cabin and raise horses and sell them to the settlers."

"Sounds like a great idea, Chief, but not with this gold. It belongs to Wells Fargo."

"It belongs to the one who has it," Dan Two Feather said.

"And right now we have it, Chief."

"We take it from you."

"Sorry, Chief. I've gone too far and suffered too much grief to let you take this here bullion."

The rifle in Dan Two Feather's hand shifted slightly so that the muzzle was pointing at Longarm's chest. There was nothing in his eyes to indicate any reluctance to do what had to be done. Longarm looked from the yawning muzzle to the chief's impassive face—and with a shrug, said nothing more.

A quick nod of the Indian's head brought the other two quickly to the wagon. They slid from their saddles, reached up and took Consuela by the arms, and pulled her none too gently down from the wagon, then clambered up into it to inspect its contents. Watching them, Longarm asked the chief if he could remove his provisions from the wagon.

Dan Two Feather nodded in agreement.

Longarm dismounted and clambered up into the ore wagon, and handed down their provisions and cooking gear to Consuela. Glancing over at the two Indians as he worked, he saw them examining in some awe the solid gold bars they were holding in their hands. Though they were obviously impressed by the gold's weight and its smooth, yellowish sheen, they appeared to be wondering how they could use them as a medium of exchange.

When he jumped down off the wagon, Consuela pulled him aside.

"Longarm," she whispered, "I know that Indian, the one you talk to."

"Dan Two Feather?"

"If that is hees name, yes!"

"How do you know him?"

"He kill Peterson. Then he ask about you. He call you gunfighter. He want to know if I have kill you."

"I already figured they've been following us."

"Why they want the gold?"

"They want to buy land and live like white men."

"Will you let them take it?"

"Right now, I don't have much choice in the matter. But I'll do what I can to talk them out of it."

"How you do that?"

"Watch."

Longarm walked over to Dan Two Feather, who was getting ready to pull himself up into the ore wagon.

"Wait a minute, Chief," Longarm said.

Dan Two Feather turned to face Longarm. "Speak, gunfighter."

"I think I better warn you."

Dan Two Feather smiled at him. "Yes, I hear what you say before. But I think we will take it anyway."

"I'm not going to stop you, Chief. Take the gold if you want. But it won't do you any good. In fact, it might bring you a hornet's nest of trouble."

"The gold is bad medicine?"

"How long you been following me, Chief?"

"Since the gunfighter killed the Mexicans."

"Well, have you counted how many men have died since then?"

The Indian nodded solemnly. "Many are dead."

"Then you know, Chief, how this gold draws trouble. But even if you can keep the gold, you can't use it. You won't be able to buy a damn thing with it. Except trouble."

"Does not the white man worship gold?"

"Yes. But not in this form. It has to be melted down, shaped into coins."

"I will find a white eyes to do this."

"You'll never find one. Besides, if any one of you turns up with a gold bar—or freshly minted gold coins, it don't matter which—the alarm will be given, and pretty soon you'll be back in Utah."

"We will see," the Indian said.

"All right, Chief," Longarm said. "Keep the gold and good luck to you. But don't say I didn't warn you."

"You will not try to stop us from taking your gold?"

"You heard what I said, Chief."

"We will take ore wagon. Stay with your woman and do not follow us. Dan Two Feather not want to kill gunfighter. We will leave horse for your woman if you do not want her to walk beside your horse, as do the women of our people."

"I think she'd rather ride, Chief."

Dan Two Feather called out in his Ute tongue to his companions in the ore wagon, then walked back to his paint, lifted the reins of Newland's dun off his saddlehorn, and let them fall to the ground, indicating with a nod that this was the horse he was leaving for Consuela. Springing into his saddle then, he snatched up his reins and gave another order to the Indians in the wagon. The one Longarm judged to be Billy Indian jumped down and hopped aboard his mount, while Joe Big Hat snatched up the team's ribbons. Riding out in front of the wagon, Dan Two Feather waved his arm. Joe Big Hat snapped the reins over the horses' backs and sent the wagon into motion.

Standing in the dust raised by their departure, Longarm

and Consuela watched the wagon rattle across the canyon floor until it disappeared into a narrow arroyo.

"What we do now?" Consuela asked wearily.

"I don't know about you. I'm going after them."

"They will kill you."

"They will try."

"I go with you. You heard the old Indian. He say I am your woman."

Longarm was too wise to argue.

"Well, now, this should do nicely," Longarm said, walking closer to the edge of the bluff.

Consuela slipped from the dun and hurried over to him as he peered down at the dusty excuse for a town below them. A two days' ride north had brought them into higher, cooler country, where the air was fresher, the valleys broad and green, the mountain slopes clad in pine. The town below them had only a general store, a livery, and a saloon. No telegraph, and no rail line. At best it served as a source of provisions and supplies for cattlemen—and amusement for their riders, eager for a blowout as they rode in from the nearby spreads they were working.

"What you mean?" Consuela asked.

He pointed at the ore wagon. It was slowing as the two Indians escorting it headed toward the town's general store. "The chief is probably going in there with a gold bar to stock up on provisions. Think I'll go down to join the party. It should be a good one."

"Hey, you crazy or something?"

He turned to her. "Look. A couple of days ago I did what I could to warn that Indian what would happen to him if he tried to cash one of those gold bars. He didn't believe me. Well, I'm going to be down there when he finds out how right I was."

"I go with you."

He handed his rifle to her. "No. I want you to stay here. Once the men in that store—or the saloon next to it—get a look at you, all bets will be off. You're too much of a distraction."

Taking the rifle, she pouted, but only a little. His words did much for her self-esteem. "Be careful, Custees."

He mounted up quickly and headed off the bluff.

As Longarm strode past the two Utes standing beside the ore wagon on his way to the general store, he saw a towheaded youngster dart from the store's side entrance and plunge excitedly into the saloon next door. Two horses were standing at the saloon's hitch rack.

Longarm entered the general store and saw Dan Two Feather pointing out to the store owner what provisions he wanted. The owner, a spare straw of a man with sleeve garters on his dingy white shirt, looked confused and frightened as he added the goods Dan Two Feather was ordering to a growing mound on his counter. The gold bar the chief had brought with him was sitting on the counter next to the scale. In the store's poor, dusty light it gleamed dully, improbably.

To Longarm's right, just inside the door, stood a cold potbelly stove with four wooden chairs sitting around it. He slumped down in one of the chairs and leaned back until its back rested against a windowsill. Folding his arms, Longarm watched the chief shop. At Longarm's entrance, the store owner had squinted hopefully at him, but at Longarm's bland, noncommital stare, he'd looked away and gone back to serving the chief. Dan Two Feather had also noted Longarm's entry, but there had not been the slightest flicker of recognition.

"A barrel of flour," the chief said, "and two sack of potatoes."

The storeowner held up, frazzled. "Look here, Mr. Indian, at this rate you ain't going to leave me no provisions to sell, and I already told you. I can't accept that gold bar."

The chief shrugged. "If you want, I take the gold bar back. But I keep the provisions."

"That's robbery!"

The chief shrugged. "Keep gold bar."

"But that bar ain't legal tender. Where'd you get it anyway?"

"I took it from the wagon."

The store owner took out a polka-dot handkerchief and mopped his brow, then the back of his neck. His eyes, Longarm noted, kept flicking in the direction of the door. He was waiting anxiously for the help that kid was supposed to bring from the saloon.

And it came before he put away his handkerchief.

A wiry cowpoke, his sixgun drawn, strode into the store and headed quickly over to the chief, covering him. He was dust-covered and his eyes were red-rimmed. He had evidently been flushing his tonsils with firewater when the youngster had burst in to tell him about the crazy Indian.

"Hi, Jeeter," the store owner said in obvious relief. "Didn't know you was in town."

"Just rode in, Mike."

Jeeter strode over to the counter and picked up the gold bar.

"I told this crazy Indian I couldn't take that for what he's buyin' here," the store owner explained. "I figure he must've stole it from a shipment."

Jeeter turned to the chief, holding the bar up to him. "Hey, redskin, where'd you get this?"

The chief said nothing.

The door opened and another cowpoke burst in. He was holding his sixgun in his hand.

"Jeeter!" he cried. "This wagon out here's loaded with gold bars!"

"Go on back outside and keep an eye on it, Sandy. Them two redskins givin' you any trouble?"

Sandy grinned. "They started to, but we stopped that quick enough."

As Sandy hurried back out, Longarm glanced out the window. The saloon's barkeep, still wearing his apron, was holding a shotgun on the two Indians.

Longarm got to his feet and strode toward Jeeter. Jeeter looked at him, eyes narrowed. "That your horse out there?"

"Yep."

Jeeter handed the bar to Longarm. "What do you think of this?"

Longarm hefted the bar, then put it down on the counter. "This here bar was stolen from a Wells Fargo shipment."

"That's likely, I guess," Jeeter replied, grinning. "But the important thing is, there's a wagon out there filled with 'em."

"What're you figuring to do?"

Jeeter grinned. "Looks like I struck it rich. A couple of these bars and I can quit ridin' fences for the rest of my life."

"Just a couple?"

"Well, no sense in getting greedy. I figure there's enough to go around for all of us."

"Not really. I just told you. That gold belongs to Wells Fargo."

"You expectin' me to take your word on that?"

"Nope."

Longarm flashed his badge and at the same time drew his .44, thrusting the sixgun's barrel into Jeeter's navel. Lowering his own sixgun, Jeeter stepped quickly back.

"Hey, no need to draw on me, Marshal."

"Fine," Longarm said. He took the gold bar off the counter and tossed it to the chief. Then he took Jeeter's sixgun from him and stuck it in his belt. "Now come on out with us and call off them other two."

"What about this Indian?"

Longarm glanced at the chief, then back at Jeeter. "He's one of my deputies."

"If he's your deputy, what was he doin' with this gold bar?"

"Just a misunderstanding. Right, Chief?"

Dan Two Feather nodded impassively.

"Well, what about these provisions?" the store owner piped up. "Ain't you goin' to buy them?"

"Load them in the wagon and tote up your bill," Longarm told him. "I'll pay for it."

"It's goin' to be expensive."

"Just add it up carefully."

"Sure. Sure."

With Jeeter in front of him, Longarm pushed out of the store, the chief beside him. "Tell Sandy and the barkeep to lower their guns," Longarm told Jeeter.

Jeeter hesitated.

"Do it! Now!"

Longarm poked the barrel of his .44 deeper into the cowpoke's back.

"Lower your guns, boys!" Jeeter cried. "It's all a mistake. This here U.S. deputy's taking that gold in."

The barkeep promptly lowered his shotgun, but the cowpoke, Sandy, seemed a bit more uncertain. He did not lower his gun as he peered incredulously at Jeeter.

"You say he's a U.S. deputy?" Sandy demanded.

"Yeah," Jeeter told him. "Do like I told you, for Christ's sake. He's got a gun in my back."

"Shit. I say he ain't no U.S. deputy. I say he just wants this gold."

It was getting sticky, and it looked for a moment as if Longarm was going to have to shoot it out with this stubborn cowpoke. That was something he absolutely did not want. Sandy and his buddy were just innocent bystanders in all this. Suddenly, from around the side of the ore wagon, stepped Consuela. She was carrying Longarm's rifle. Before Jeeter could warn him, she had thrust the rifle's muzzle into Sandy's side.

"Drop the gun, gringo!"

The sharp prod of the rifle barrel drained the fight out of Sandy. He dropped his sixgun to the ground. The barkeep dropped his shotgun as well.

"Thanks, Consuela," Longarm said, when he reached her. "But I told you to wait back there."

"I do what I want, Custees," she told him. "You not know that yet?"

"I know it."

Longarm took the gold bar back from Dan Two Feather and tossed it into the wagon, then picked up the two guns and flung them into it as well.

"We'll leave your weapons on the trace outside of town," Longarm told Jeeter and the others.

"That's real decent of you, Marshal."

"Just don't get any ideas about coming after me. That gold is Wells Fargo property."

"All right. All right. I might have figured something like that."

The two cowpokes and the barkeep backed up, then turned and trudged back to the saloon.

Longarm and the three Indians returned to the store. Longarm paid for the provisions Dan Two Feather had already selected with a government voucher and helped them carry the goods back out to where the ore wagon sat. Longarm pointed out that even when Consuela returned the dun to the chief, they would have difficulty packing all these provisions on their horses, since Longarm would be using the wagon to take the gold back.

Dan Two Feather said nothing, and the three Indians quickly loaded their own horses and the two packhorses. It turned out they were only forced to leave behind one of the two sacks of potatoes. This sack Longarm shouldered into the ore wagon. Billy Indian and Joe Big Hat mounted up, but before Dan Two Feather did, he walked over to Longarm.

"We go now," he announced.

"Where you headed, Chief?"

"We go north, to the land of the red jackets."

"Canada?"

"If that is what the place is called."

"You'll run into a lot of Blackfeet there."

"We are match for any Blackfeet," he said, thrusting his chest out slightly. "And it will be better land than this, a shining land. If we stay here, the soldiers will come to bring us back to agency. But we are blanket Indian no more." He looked keenly then at Longarm. "What gunfighter say before is true. This gold is bad medicine for Indian. Take it and go in peace."

"Thanks, Chief."

The Indian turned abruptly, mounted up, and leading his two companions, rode out of town. A pleased grin on her face, Consuela climbed back into the ore wagon and took up the reins. With Longarm riding alongside, the ore wagon rumbled out of town. As he had promised, he had Consuela throw out the barkeep's shotgun and the cowpokes sixguns.

A week later, they arrived in Red Horse.

Chapter 12

As Longarm kept abreast of the ore wagon, he counted at least six troopers on Red Horse's sidewalks. When he and Consuela pulled up in front of the Wells Fargo Express office at the train depot, he saw the troop had set up its camp in a field on the other side of the tracks.

Dismounting, he looked up at Consuela. "You can come into the express office with me or stay out here."

"I go in with you."

He took Consuela's hand as she jumped down beside him and they walked into the Wells Fargo office. A pleasant-looking man in a starched, striped shirt with black sleeve garters was behind the counter. He greeted Longarm, then nodded pleasantly to Consuela. Without preamble, Longarm took out his badge and flashed it at the clerk.

"I'm Custis Long," he told him. "I got some gold bullion outside belongs to Wells Fargo. I want to ship it back to the Denver mint."

"Bullion, you say? How much?"

"I haven't been able to check it out for sure yet, but there's supposed to be one hundred thousand dollars worth."

"Did you say one hundred thousand?"

"I did."

"Well, now," the clerk said, doing his best to put a cork on his astonishment. "I guess we'd better get that gold right in here."

"My thinking exactly."

The clerk called two husky youngsters from the back and went out with them to oversee the unloading. Longarm and Consuela went with them. The clerk and his two helpers were unable to fit more than a few bars in the Wells Fargo safe, and ended up piling most of the bars against the wall next to the safe. After an uneasy glance at the gleaming bullion, the clerk mopped his perspiring brow and turned to Longarm.

"I must tell you, Marshal, I am not at all comfortable leaving all this bullion out in plain sight."

"Me neither," said Longarm. "What about these troopers here in town? What are they doing here?"

"They're after some Utes jumped their reservation. And some pesky banditos been robbing the ore wagons. They'd be on their way now, but the town's been kind of wild since Sheriff Newland took after his deputy."

"You haven't got a town constable?"

"He quit as soon as the sheriff rode out, I am afraid."

"Well, if you're waiting for Newland and his deputy to return, forget it."

"Why would you say that, sir?"

"They're both dead."

"You know that for a fact?"

"For a fact."

The man's eyebrows knitted. "Well, then. That is very disturbing news. I guess the town council better elect a new sheriff. And soon."

"I guess you better. Now, when's the earliest you can ship out this bullion?"

"Ten-thirty tomorrow morning—the next train through to Denver."

"Good. I'll go over and talk to the cavalry. Maybe the captain can spare a few men to guard this gold overnight."

"That's a very good idea, Marshal. I hope the captain will be willing to help us."

As Longarm started from the office, he was halted by Consuela's urgent tugging on his sleeve. He turned to her. She was frowning peevishly at him.

"Hey," she said, "when does Consuela get her money?"

Longarm turned back to the clerk. "The lady here is expecting her reward for helping me locate the gold," he explained. "Can you issue her a Wells Fargo draft for a part of the amount?"

Startled at the request, the clerk looked quickly at Consuela, then back at Longarm. "My word, no. I have no such authority. I'm afraid that will have to wait until the bullion is delivered to the Wells Fargo authorities in Denver. Any reward would be up to them. And that should take a while, I imagine."

Longarm looked back at Consuela and shrugged. "I'm sorry, Consuela."

Furious, she spun about and stalked from the express office.

Outside, he caught up with her in front of the ore wagon. Her dark face was enough to bring rain, but he did his best to ignore it.

"Don't be unreasonable, Consuela," he told her. "All this means is that you'll have to come to Denver with me. Relax. I'll show you a good time. That's a promise."

"Denver it ees long way. How do I know I will get the money then?"

"You have my word, Consuela."

"I want more than your word."

"Tell you what I'll do. I'll send Vail a telegram. I'll ask him to verify that you'll get your reward when we get to Denver."

"Vail is beeg man?"

"He's the U.S. marshal for this whole territory."

"All right. I wait for his telegram."

Longarm reached into his pocket. "Here," he said, dropping some silver into her hand. "Go buy yourself a change of clothing and maybe a bath, then check in at the hotel. I might be a while."

As she looked down at the money gleaming in her palm, her disposition improved dramatically. Eyes wide, she looked up at him.

"Where you go now?"

"I've got to return this wagon. Then I'm going over to see the officer in charge of this cavalry troop, see about him lending us some troopers to keep the gold under guard overnight." He smiled at her. "Remember, if that gold gets away, there goes your reward."

Obviously feeling much better, Consuela impulsively flung her arms around his neck and kissed him full on the lips, then turned and hurried off toward the town's main street.

Pleased with her new blouse and skirt, scrubbed clean, her hair washed and combed out to its full length, Consuela was whirling delightedly in front of the dresser mirror when she heard a light tap on her door.

She turned to the door, a frown on her face. If it were Longarm, he would not rap like that—he would stride in without knocking. Another light rap, slightly more urgent this time, came again. She walked over to the door and halted in front of it.

"Who is it?"

"Pedro!" he whispered. "Let me in!" he said in Spanish.

Pedro?

She opened the door. Pedro slipped in quickly and closed the door behind him, a nervous, yet triumphant smile on his face. His eyes sat in dark hollows. He looked thin, sunken-cheeked, like one who had slept for a time with the Angel of Death, she thought.

"Pedro," she said in a hushed voice, adding also in Spanish, "You look very bad."

Pedro shrugged fatalistically. "You should've seen me when I had a hole in my chest. I'm a hell of a lot better than I was, and I'm good enough for what's ahead."

The intensity in his hoarse voice alarmed her. What was he planning to do? she wondered. She edged backward until she reached the bed and slumped down onto it. "Why are you here now?"

"I'm after the gold. You brought it here, did you not?"

"Yes. The Wells Fargo clerk has it in his office."

He grinned. "Well, that's all right," he told her. "We'll just have to take it back."

"We?"

"You and me—and a little help from a few others."

"But Longarm is going to get the troopers to guard the gold. And then tomorrow they will put it on the train to Denver."

"Don't worry. We won't be going near it tonight."

"When, then?"

"On the train."

"What do you want me to do?"

"Listen to me. There's a steep grade about twenty miles out of town. At the top of that grade, we'll stop the train and unload the gold onto packhorses."

"You make it sound so easy."

"Hell, woman, I know it won't be easy. But I'll be on the train to help you take care of Longarm and the mail clerk and anyone else who might try to stop us."

He took a small, ivory-handled Smith and Wesson from his belt and handed it to her.

"It's loaded," he told her. "Keep it hid and when the train halts, use it if you have to if Longarm tries to stop us."

"You want me to kill Longarm?" She was amazed.

"Kill him, wound him. Shoot off his balls. I don't care. But I might need you to keep him off me when I enter the baggage car and when I'm helping load the pack horses."

She looked down at the small, gleaming revolver, her thoughts racing as she tried to decide if Pedro's was the best course of action for her. It did not take her long to decide. This way, if she and Pedro took the gold, she would get much more than the pitiful reward promised her by Longarm. This settled it for her. She glanced up at Pedro.

"Afterward, Pedro, will you take me to San Francisco?"

"Better than that," he told her. "You wait. I have a very big surprise for you."

He moved quickly to the door, pulled it open, stepped out, and vanished.

Captain Billings ushered Longarm into his tent. The two men sat down in canvas-backed camp chairs, facing each other. Longarm, long since out of cheroots, gratefully accepted one from the captain. After they lighted up, the captain asked Longarm what he could do for him.

"Guard my gold," Longarm responded.

"What's that? Gold?"

"Gold bullion to be exact. One hundred thousand worth."

The captain whistled. "You want to give me a few more details?"

Longarm explained the situation, careful, however, to omit any mention of the Utes. When he was done, both cheroots were down to stubs. Billings handed Longarm another cheroot and unwrapped one for himself.

"You've sure had a hellish time, Marshal."

"Like I said, gold attracts all manner of men."

"It did help settle California, at that," the man agreed. "Now, what you want me to do is detail some men to guard that express office until you can load the bullion onto the train tomorrow morning."

"That's it."

"How many men do you think it would take?"

"I'll leave that up to you."

The captain considered for a moment, then said, "I'd put two outside the express office—in plain sight, and keep one inside the office—as a hole card, sort of."

"Sounds good to me, Captain."

"Before you go, I have a question."

"Go ahead."

"From what you just said, you've done us all a service by taking out them banditos—but you didn't mention sighting any Utes. Did you?"

"I came on a few. But they were heading south."

"Heading south, you say?"

"Yeah. To join Geronimo in Mexico."

"In that case, I'll alert General Miles."

Longarm chuckled. "You think he's ever goin' to corner Geronimo?"

"Sure, given another ten years."

Both men laughed.

"I'll see to that guard detail within the hour, Marshal."

"I appreciate it, Captain."

Longarm stood up, the two men shook hands, and Longarm left. He walked back across the tracks and dropped into the telegraph office. In his telegram to Vail, he advised him of his plans and asked him to verify that Consuela would be assured of her reward. After he sent the telegram, he told the telegrapher that any reply from Vail was to be delivered promptly to him at the hotel.

After a celebratory dinner with Consuela in the hotel's dining room—he topped off the three-course dinner with a glass of port—Longarm escorted Consuela up to their room, filled with the satisfaction that comes with the prospect of a difficult mission near completion. Surprised and delighted—and certainly aroused—at Consuela's seeming reluctance to let him take her, he playfully examined her new blouse and dress, and in the act, disrobed her. A moment later, unashamedly naked himself, he pressed her gently down onto the bed, his teeth teasing her right earlobe, his big hand caressing her beasts.

Soon, all reluctance gone, Consuela answered his embraces with a savage embrace of her own, and they spent the next few hours pounding at each other like beasts in the wood, then teasing and arousing each other until it seemed their hunger for each other was inexhaustible. At last, spent completely, Longarm rolled over and promptly dropped into a deep, untroubled sleep.

Consuela lay on her back, staring up at the ceiling, her thoughts in a turmoil. At last, unable to hold herself back any longer, she poked Longarm violently with her elbow, then teased and pulled on him until she had retrieved him from the deep sleep into which he had fallen.

"What?" he muttered, his eyes flickering open. "Ain't you had enough?"

"Custees, tell me," she hissed, "why you not kiss Consuela?"

"Kiss you?"

"On the lips . . . why you not kiss Consuela on the lips?"

He groaned in utter exasperation. "Go to sleep, Consuela."

He started to turn over, away from her. She would not let him. Grabbing his shoulder, she yanked him back around, forcing him to face her.

"Just now, we make love. But you not kiss me on the lips. And before this you never do it, not once. I remember."

"Jesus," Longarm sighed wearily.

"Is it because you not supposed to kiss a whore on the lips?" she persisted.

"What the hell?"

"Answer me. Is that why?"

Longarm rolled over and yanked the sheets angrily up over his shoulder. "Go to sleep, Consuela," he muttered. "We got a big day tomorrow."

Consuela turned angrily away and let him fall back to sleep. He had not denied what she said. Instead, he had turned his back on her. It was true what she thought. To him, she was a whore. That was why he never kissed her on the lips.

Tears coursing down her cheeks, she stared miserably up at the ceiling. It was a long time before she turned on her side, ducked her head onto the wet pillow, and slept.

Chapter 13

After their breakfast in the hotel, Longarm leaned close to Consuela and caught her gaze. It had been a quiet breakfast and Consuela had seemed unusually evasive. Longarm leaned over and took her hand.

"You mind telling me what that was all about last night?"

"It was nothing," she replied. "Forget it. I was tired."

"Come on. Out with it. I was the one who was tired, too tired to listen. But I'm wide awake now, so tell me."

"I already tell you, it was nothing," she replied stubbornly.

"Didn't seem like it, Consuela."

She shrugged. "I jus' ask why you not kiss me on the lips."

He released her hand and leaned back in his chair, cocking his head as he peered at her. "Now why in the hell would you ask me a thing like that?"

"It is nothing, I tell you. You do not have to kiss me, Longarm. I understand."

"You understand nothing, Consuela—if you're thinking what I think you're thinking."

"It does not matter."

"Stand up now and I'll kiss you—right in front of everybody."

He reached out to take her hand again, but she yanked it back, her face flushed in embarrassment. Then she looked quickly around at the other diners. "Custees! Please! You must not do such a thing!"

Longarm laughed. "Later then."

The hotel's desk clerk appeared at Longarm's elbow. He was holding a yellow envelope in his hand. "Marshal Long?"

"Yes?"

"Telegram."

"Thanks."

As Longarm took the envelope, he glanced at the table at Consuela. "Maybe this is that reward verification I asked Vail to send."

"Read it," she said.

He tore open the envelope and pulled out the telegram:

CUSTIS LONG
RED HORSE COLORADO

REWARD OF ONE PERCENT OF TOTAL RECOVERED BULLION WILL BE AWARDED CONSUELA IN CERTIFIED WELLS FARGO DRAFT IN DENVER STOP ORTEGA

WOUNDED NOT KILLED IN YUMA ESCAPE STOP NOW
AT LARGE STOP TAKE NO CHANCES END MESSAGE

MARSHAL BILLY VAIL
FEDERAL DISTRICT COURT
DENVER COLORADO

"Well," Consuela asked. "What do your boss say?"

"I'll read it to you," Longarm told her. " 'Reward of one percent of total recovered bullion will be awarded Consuela in certified Wells Fargo draft in Denver.' "

"One percent? What ees this one percent?"

Longarm folded the telegram and pocketed it. "I figure that should come out close to one thousand dollars."

"One thousand dollars? For all that much gold bars?"

"That's a pretty hefty amount."

"Maybe *you* think so."

"Damn it, Consuela, that's close to what I make in a full year."

"It ees nothing, I tell you!"

Longarm shrugged, dropped some coins on the table, and stood up. "No sense in arguing about it," he told her. "Come on, we got to see to the loading of that gold. The train's due in less than an hour."

A determined pout on her face, Consuela got up and allowed Longarm to escort her from the restaurant.

After they finished loading the gold bars into the baggage car, Longarm and the captain enjoyed a quiet smoke together on the express office's porch until it was time for the train to pull out. Then they escorted Consuela across the station platform to the train. Reaching it, Longarm turned to the captain and shook his hand.

"You've been a great help, Captain," Longarm told him. "I appreciate it."

"As I just said, Longarm, the only scare my men had guarding that bullion was when them coyotes started howling in the hills."

"Will your troop be pulling out now?"

"I've been told to remain in Red Horse until the locals can elect a new sheriff and deputy."

"Good luck, then."

The captain turned to Consuela and touched the tip of his hat to her. "It's been a pleasure, ma'am," he said. "I hope you have a pleasant trip."

"Thank you, Captain," Consuela replied, just a little flustered by this Southern officer's gallant manner.

Taking Consuela's arm, Longarm escorted her up the steps into the train. They had tickets for a seats in the first car behind the mail and baggage car. Longarm took a moment to glance around at the other passengers before folding his long frame down beside Consuela.

"Who you look for?" she asked, frowning.

"Just checkin'," he told her, "looking for any familiar faces. Word of all that bullion we're carrying might've gotten out."

"We have only been in this town overnight. I think you crazy to worry now."

He looked at her sharply. "Do you?"

"*Sí.* Of course."

"Well, I'll keep my eyes open anyway—just in case."

"Suit yourself."

She seemed unusually jumpy, a fact that did not escape his notice. He unwrapped a fresh cheroot and stuck it in his mouth without lighting it, tipped his hat forward, and leaned back against the seat. The conductor sang out, announcing the train's imminent departure. A few late passengers, holding carpetbags or valises in front of them, stepped up into the train and hurried down the aisle, looking for seats. There was a distant hoot from the engine, the train rocked, halted, then started up again, and in a moment they were rolling out of the station, slowly building speed, heading east for Denver.

When the train slowed, then stopped completely a few miles out of Red Horse to take on water, Longarm unfolded his long frame and stood up.

Consuela reached up and took his arm. "Where you go now?"

"I think I'll just check out our shipment," he told her. "I get nervous whenever this train slows or stops—for whatever reason."

"I go with you."

"No need for that. Stay here in your seat."

"It is my gold, don't forget. I do not want to lose my reward."

"Even if it's only one thousand dollars?"

"It's better than nothing—I think."

He smiled at her. "You think right. Come along then."

The conductor was just pulling the baggage car's sliding door shut when Longarm entered. As the train started up again, the conductor sat down to finish his checker game with the mail clerk. They'd set up the checkerboard on top of a nail keg, and were sitting around it on wooden folding chairs.

Longarm looked around the baggage car. Chickens clucked unhappily in an open crate in the forward section of the car, and close around them were piled kegs of flour, apples, sugar, and other foodstuffs. Crated boxes, all with the familiar Wells Fargo Express tag, were stacked clear to the ceiling. The mail had already been sorted into their cubicles on the wall, and two huge canvas mail sacks were piled next to the Wells Fargo safe. On the other side of it, the piles of gold bullion were stacked neatly.

"See?" said Consuela, her eyes on the gold. "You worry for nothing."

"Maybe so," said Longarm, walking over to watch the two checker players.

The mail clerk looked up from the board at Longarm. "Hi, Marshal."

"Who's winning?"

"I am," he replied, and as Longarm watched, he executed a neat triple jump to end the game.

With a sigh the conductor got to his feet. "You planning on stayin' in here, Marshal?" he asked Longarm.

"For a while, anyway."

"There's a folding chair over in that corner for the lady."

He glanced at his watch, and with a brisk nod to Longarm and Consuela, left the car.

"Maybe you'd care to play?" the mail clerk asked Longarm hopefully.

"Sure thing."

Longarm brought over a chair for Consuela to sit in, then sat down in the conductor's chair and pushed a checker forward into battle. Three games later, every one of which he had lost, he noticed the train slowing on a steep grade. He held his finger on the checker he was about to move and looked up to see a gaunt, barely recognizable Pedro burst into the baggage car. Pedro held his sixgun in his right hand, the conductor in front of him with his left.

As the conductor struggled to free himself, Pedro clubbed him to the floor with a single, vicious blow from his sixgun. On his feet by that time, Longarm flung his chair at the Mexican, striking him in the side of his head. Pedro rocked back, stumbled, and fell. Before Longarm could draw his .44, Consuela rammed a small Smith and Wesson into his right side.

"Drop your gun," she told him.

Longarm stared at her. He was not surprised—just saddened. He dropped his revolver.

Kicking the chair out of his way, Pedro scrambled to his feet. "How you like this, gringo," he cried, grinning. "Now drop that damn belly gun."

Longarm unclipped the derringer from his watch chain and dropped it to the floor beside the Colt. Pedro stepped forward and kicked both weapons into a corner. Then he turned his attention to the mail clerk. On Pedro's entrance, the clerk had leaped away from the nail keg, and now cowered against the wall.

"Come over here and open the safe," Pedro told him. "Don't make any sudden moves and you won't get hurt."

The man nodded eagerly, his face white with terror. He scuttled over to the safe and with trembling hands began to work the combination. The train's wheels squealed suddenly, then locked, skidding over the steel rails as the train ground to a halt.

Pedro moved over to the sliding door. "Keep the bastard covered," he told Consuela.

Lifting the latch, Pedro shoved aside the door. A riderless horse was standing close by the baggage car. The horse's rider, Longarm assumed, was now in the train's cab, his gun leveled on the engineer and fireman. Mexican horsemen leading a line of pack horses came in sight then, galloping up to the train.

In a moment they reached the train and clambered up into the car. At sight of the gold, they cheered, took off their sombreros, and slapped their thighs. Then, working themselves into a happy sweat, they transferred the bullion onto their packhorses, and had just finished cleaning out the Wells Fargo safe when the train began to creep forward. The Mexicans jumped off the train, mounted their horses, and led their loaded packhorses away from the train.

Standing in front of the open door, Pedro cocked his gun and aimed at Longarm. As he did so, he glanced at Consuela.

"Get over here," he told her. "Now you see that surprise I promise for you."

As he spoke, Ortega Gasset swung up onto a riderless horse. It was he, Longarm realized, who had halted the train.

"Consuela!" he called into the car. "Come with me!"

"Ortega!" Consuela cried. "Is it you?"

"What you think?"

"But they say you are dead."

"I think maybe they lie," he called in to her, a wide grin on his face. "Hurry! There is room on thees horse. Jump on!"

The train's speed was increasing. Consuela hesitated.

"Hurry up," Pedro told her, his gun still trained on Longarm. "Get out of here while I take care of this gringo."

Consuela swung around to face him. "You shoot heem?"

"Sure. Why not?"

"No!"

"I already do it," he said, pulling the trigger.

But even as the detonation filled the baggage car, Consuela had lunged at Longarm, shoving him out of the bullet's path. Gasping in pain, she collapsed to the floor of the car. Longarm flung himself at the astonished Pedro, yanked the gun from his grasp, and sent two quick rounds into his chest. As Pedro toppled backward out of the car, Ortega cursed, swung his horse around, and galloped away from the train. Longarm tracked him and fired. The outlaw slumped forward over his mount's neck, but hung on and was soon out of range.

Longarm dropped beside Consuela. She was looking up at him, wide-eyed.

"Where you hit?" Longarm asked.

"My side. It feel like someone punch me."

The train was over the crest now, gaining speed rapidly. Through the baggage car's still-open door, Longarm saw the outlaws approaching a low ridge. Suddenly a line of troopers appeared on its crest. Firing their rifles over the outlaws' heads to warn them, the troopers charged. The outlaws reined to a halt and flung up their hands.

Longarm looked back down at Consuela. Her eyes were closed. Lifting her side slightly, he saw a gout of blood pulsing from her wound. She had taken Pedro's bullet under her right breast. As he brushed her dark hair off her forehead, she opened her eyes.

"Now you kiss Consuela on the lips?" she asked.

He kissed her full on the lips. She responded with her old passion, and for a moment he had the illusion she was going to be fine—that her wound had been superficial, but all too soon her lips lost their warmth. He felt a shudder travel the length of her. Releasing her lips, he sat back and gazed down into her once-luminous eyes.

They were frozen open in death.

Chapter 14

Vail shouldered up to the bar beside Longarm. Longarm glanced over at him.

"Hi, Billy. What're you drinking?"

"Nothin' right now. I been lookin' all over for you. You been out of touch for more'n a week."

"I quit, Chief."

"Bullshit."

"You're right. It's bullshit. What I'm doin' is, I'm takin' a vacation."

"That's all right with me. Take all the time you need."

"That's decent of you, Billy."

"Hey, can we find a booth? I want to talk to you."

"What're you drinking?" Longarm asked again.

"I told you. Nothin'."

"Go to hell then."

"All right. All right. Beer."

Longarm ordered a beer for Vail, and when it came,

he took his bottle and shot glass with him and led the way over to an empty booth.

"How come you're drinkin' so hard?" Vail asked Longarm as he squeezed himself into the seat opposite him.

"I'm trying to stop smoking," Longarm replied, pouring himself a fresh shot. "So far it's worked fine. Haven't had a smoke since the day before yesterday."

Billy said nothing in reply and sipped his beer for a while. Watching him warily, Longarm filled his shot glass and sipped it. After a moment or two, Vail cleared his throat.

"There's something I been meaning to ask you," Vail said.

"What's that?"

"How'd you know where to plant them cavalrymen?"

"A guess, that's all. It was close to Red Horse and the grade was steep enough to slow the train to a crawl. That's what the stationmaster in Red Horse told me. And I knew if Ortega was going to take back his gold, that would be as good a spot as any. He sure as hell couldn't take it from us in Denver."

"Yeah. Well, it was a shrewd guess and worked out well."

"Not for Consuela."

"You know what I meant, Custis."

"Yeah. I know what you meant." Longarm frowned with sudden intensity at Vail. "Hard to figure, isn't it, Billy? When it came to getting what she wanted, Consuela was ruthless. She sliced a young Mexican's throat in cold blood with my pocket knife, and I found the same pocket knife in Newland's back before he died.

And she wanted that gold as much as anyone on this earth. But she saved my life without a thought of her own. I can't figure it."

"Don't try."

"What the hell's that supposed to mean?"

"It means you can never know what a woman will do—or why. And you shouldn't try. You might as well try to predict which way the wind'll blow next Tuesday."

Vail sat back then and said nothing more. After a short while, Longarm shoved aside the nearly empty whiskey bottle and reached into his side pocket and took out a cheroot. He unwrapped it carefully, thoughtfully. When he bit off the tip, Vail flicked a match to life and lit the cheroot. Once Longarm got it going to his satisfaction, he smiled wearily at Vail. "So much for breaking the habit."

"You know what Mark Twain says. It's easy to stop smoking. He's done it hundreds of times."

Longarm leaned back and drew reflectively on the cheroot. "Think of it, Billy. So many lives down the drain—all them crazy people after the gold. Not only Consuela and Ortega, but Newland too. And those banditos. Even them Utes."

"You figured out why, have you?"

"Yeah, but it wasn't me thought of it. One of them banditos I took down told me that without gold, life was one long constipation."

"That's a drastic way to put it, I admit."

"But that's damn close to it. Money is power, Billy—and to people without power, its the only chance they'll ever have to get up off the mat."

"Does that mean you want a raise?"

Longarm smiled wanly. "Now that you mention it, a hundred dollars a month doesn't go very far these days."

"I'll see what I can do."

There was an awkward silence then. Vail seemed about to say something, but he held back and stared nervously into his beer. Longarm peered at him closely.

"All right. Out with it, Billy. What'd you come here to tell me?"

"I got a check here for you."

"A check?"

"A draft from Wells Fargo. The reward for returning the gold."

"You know federal marshals can't take any reward."

"Washington made an exception."

"You got the draft with you?"

"Right here." Vail patted his side pocket.

"Then shove it up your ass."

Vail took a healthy belt of his beer, then closed one eye and peered at Longarm. "I know how you feel, Custis. But I was thinkin' you could use the money—not for yourself, but maybe to put a stone or something over Consuela's grave. With that much, you could find something real nice. And the rest you could send to Ortega Gasset in Yuma. He'll be recovered soon and in that hole he could use the money."

"I hear he got life this time."

"That's right."

Longarm took a drag on his cheroot and said nothing as he considered Vail's suggestion.

"So? What about it?" Vail prodded.

Longarm allowed himself a smile. "Guess maybe that's not such a bad idea after all, Billy."

"Then you'll take the check?"

"I'll take it, but I'll need you to give me a hand picking out the stone for Consuela—and maybe you could help me with what to put on it."

"Be glad to."

Vail shoved the Wells Fargo draft across the table. Longarm picked it up, glanced at the amount, and folded and pocketed it.

"Come on, Billy," Longarm said abruptly, almost cheerfully. "Let's get the hell out of here."

The two friends left the booth and walked out of the saloon together into the bright afternoon sun.

Watch for

LONGARM AND THE COLORADO GUNDOWN

154th in the bold LONGARM series
from Jove

Coming in October!

LONGARM

Explore the exciting Old West with one of the men who made it wild!

_LONGARM AND THE VIGILANTES #140	0-515-10385-3/$2.95
_LONGARM IN THE OSAGE STRIP #141	0-515-10401-9/$2.95
_LONGARM AND THE LOST MINE #142	0-515-10426-4/$2.95
_LONGARM AND THE LONGLEY LEGEND #143	0-515-10445-0/$2.95
_LONGARM AND THE DEAD MAN'S BADGE #144	0-515-10472-8/$2.95
_LONGARM AND THE KILLER'S SHADOW #145	0-515-10494-9/$2.95
_LONGARM AND THE MONTANA MASSACRE #146	0-515-10512-0/$2.95
_LONGARM IN THE MEXICAN BADLANDS #147	0-515-10526-0/$2.95
_LONGARM AND THE BOUNTY HUNTRESS #148	0-515-10547-3/$2.95
_LONGARM AND THE DENVER BUST-OUT #149	0-515-10570-8/$2.95
_LONGARM AND THE SKULL CANYON GANG #150	0-515-10597-X/$2.95
_LONGARM AND THE RAILROAD TO HELL #151	0-515-10613-5/$3.50
_LONGARM AND THE LONE STAR CAPTIVE (Giant novel)	0-515-10646-1/$4.50
_LONGARM AND THE RIVER OF DEATH #152	0-515-10649-6/$3.50

For Visa, MasterCard and American Express orders ($10 minimum) call: 1-800-631-8571

FOR MAIL ORDERS: CHECK BOOK(S). FILL OUT COUPON. SEND TO:	POSTAGE AND HANDLING: $1.50 for one book, 50¢ for each additional. Do not exceed $4.50.
BERKLEY PUBLISHING GROUP 390 Murray Hill Pkwy., Dept. B East Rutherford, NJ 07073	BOOK TOTAL $ ____
	POSTAGE & HANDLING $ ____
NAME _____	APPLICABLE SALES TAX $ ____ (CA, NJ, NY, PA)
ADDRESS _____	
CITY _____	TOTAL AMOUNT DUE $ ____
STATE _____ ZIP _____	PAYABLE IN US FUNDS. (No cash orders accepted.)
PLEASE ALLOW 6 WEEKS FOR DELIVERY. PRICES ARE SUBJECT TO CHANGE WITHOUT NOTICE.	201e

A special offer for people who enjoy reading the best Westerns published today. If you enjoyed this book, subscribe now and get...

TWO FREE

A $5.90 VALUE—NO OBLIGATION

If you enjoyed this book and would like to read more of the very best Westerns being published today, you'll want to subscribe to True Value's Western Home Subscription Service. If you enjoyed the book you just read and want more of the most exciting, adventurous, action packed Westerns, subscribe now.

Each month the editors of True Value will select the 6 very best Westerns from America's leading publishers for special readers like you. You'll be able to preview these new titles as soon as they are published, FREE for ten days with no obligation.

TWO FREE BOOKS

When you subscribe, we'll send you your first month's shipment of the newest and best 6 Westerns for you to preview. With your first shipment, two of these books will be yours as our introductory gift to you absolutely FREE, regardless of what you decide to do. If you like them, as much as we think you will, keep all six books but pay for just 4 at the low subscriber rate of just $2.45 each. If you decide to return them, keep 2 of the titles as our gift. No obligation.

Special Subscriber Savings

When you become a True Value subscriber you'll save money several ways. First, all regular monthly selections will be billed at the low subscriber price of just $2.45 each. That's

WESTERNS!

at least a savings of $3.00 each month below the publishers price. Second, there is never any shipping, handling or other hidden charges—Free home delivery. What's more there is no minimum number of books you must buy, you may return any selection for full credit and you can cancel your subscription at any time. A TRUE VALUE!

Mail the coupon below

To start your subscription and receive 2 FREE WESTERNS, fill out the coupon below and mail it today. We'll send your first shipment which includes 2 FREE BOOKS as soon as we receive it.

Mail To: 10669
True Value Home Subscription Services, Inc.
P.O. Box 5235
120 Brighton Road
Clifton, New Jersey 07015-5235

YES! I want to start receiving the very best Westerns being published today. Send me my first shipment of 6 Westerns for me to preview FREE for 10 days. If I decide to keep them, I'll pay for just 4 of the books at the low subscriber price of $2.45 each; a total of $9.80 (a $17.70 value). Then each month I'll receive the 6 newest and best Westerns to preview Free for 10 days. If I'm not satisfied I may return them within 10 days and owe nothing. Otherwise I'll be billed at the special low subscriber rate of $2.45 each; a total of $14.70 (at least a $17.70 value) and save $3.00 off the publishers price. There are never any shipping, handling or other hidden charges. I understand I am under no obligation to purchase any number of books and I can cancel my subscription at any time, no questions asked. In any case the 2 FREE books are mine to keep.

Name _____

Address _____ Apt. # _____

City _____ State _____ Zip _____

Telephone # _____

Signature _____
(if under 18 parent or guardian must sign)
Terms and prices subject to change.
Orders subject to acceptance by True Value Home Subscription Services, Inc.